DON'T DIG TOO DEEP

Don't Dig Too Deep

MARILYN FREEMAN

Chapter 1

Although Old Saint Paul's church had stood for a thousand years, it had fallen into disrepair after the village migrated into the valley when the land around it had been cleared during the Enclosures. Rather than out of any higher motive, the Lord of the Manor of Lyngrave had commissioned a new church to be built down by the river to encourage his tenants to move to the new location. Over the intervening century and a half, the building had gradually disintegrated and was now simply a ruin standing on the hilltop above Little Stretford, merely a monument to an earlier age. The surrounding graveyard was allowed to remain. Out of respect, the area had occasionally been mown by the parishioners, although many of the gravestones were leaning at precarious angles. As far as was known, no new burials had been added after the closure of the church.

Dr Meera Carter had proposed the field adjacent to this site as the summer project for her third-year archaeology degree students. There were several interesting features to excavate, which would offer valuable practical experience. As it was situated to the north of the church just beyond the graveyard, she had little trouble obtaining the necessary licences and permissions for the excavation. In fact, it was a previously investigated site, and Meera knew exactly who had run the initial excavation. It had been her late father, Professor Robert Carter.

He had graduated from UCL with a first - class honours archaeology degree in 1970, and after achieving his Masters, and a PhD, enjoyed several years working for the Ministry of Defence, supervising the excavation of the war dead in various sites around the world.

As an only child, Meera had always been close to her father. She was a bright child, eager to learn, and as she grew up, he was only too pleased to share his passion for archaeology with her. She had spent hours with him exploring ancient sites, monuments, or churches, and it just seemed natural that she too should study the subject. In the event, her grades hadn't been good enough to secure a place at UCL and she'd had to be satisfied with studying at Bristol.

Her father had been rather disappointed that she hadn't quite been able to follow in his academic footsteps. However, she was determined to make him proud of her and worked hard hoping to get a first-class degree, as he had done. Once again, he had been disappointed that she could only manage a second-class degree, and Meera knew it. She couldn't help feeling second best.

Driven by her need to live up to his expectations, she studied for her MA and then her PhD, but unfortunately, he had died suddenly four years ago. Meera was distraught when he passed away. He had been everything to her, her inspiration, and her motivation. Sadly, he never witnessed her achievement of attaining a doctorate, and perhaps this was one reason it had seemed so fitting that her first project should be the one he had managed, a kind of tribute to him and also to show him she had finally achieved academic success.

Her mother had died of cancer five years earlier and as she had no siblings, she was now alone. She had never met her Indian family. In fact, they were never even spoken of and as Meera grew older, she had begun to realise there must have been some kind of rift between her mother and her own family. She promised herself that one day, she would find them and discover her roots.

Well, here she was, now running her own project and as she stood looking up at the ruined church, couldn't help feeling rather excited. Even though it was ostensibly to provide experience for the students, she knew that in this game, a dig could literally unearth anything. This was the thrill of archaeology and what had attracted Meera to it at her father's knee. You never knew what the next scoop of earth would reveal. Of course, often there was little or nothing, just a stain in the soil or a fragment of pottery, but as her knowledge and experience grew, she had gained more understanding of the clues the earth was giving up. However small and apparently insignificant to the untrained eye, to Meera, each clue would conjure up a picture of the person who had made it, dropped it, or simply discarded it all those years ago, even though centuries may have passed.

She had three field assistants with her on the project. Josh, Pete, and Celine. They were supervising eighteen eager third year students, and everyone was as keen as Meera to get on with the dig. They wasted little time erecting the tent in the centre of the ruined church. The roof had long since fallen in and the debris removed. Parts of the walls had also been plundered, no doubt for building materials.

Calling to them all to gather round, Meera began by running through the Site Induction, laying down the ground rules and Health and Safety information, then went on to outline the purpose of the project.

'You all know why we're here, but just so everyone's clear, our main aim is to define the exact location of a medieval building that we know once stood to the north of this church, and to discover its purpose.'

The students, under Meera's guidance, had already compiled a Desk Based Assessment, studying existing historical documents including her father's report compiled thirty-five years ago, which she had scanned and saved in her computer, and also the geophysical data generated by surveying the site with the various state of the art techniques available. The combination of all this information had given some indication as to the nature and position of features beneath the surface.

Taking out a copy of an old map from her briefcase, she laid it on the finds table and invited them all to take a look.

'This is the seventeenth century map, showing the village as it was at that time. As you can see, most of the dwellings are situated to the south of the church, with what appears to be a large building beyond the graveyard, to the north. It's possible that this building was a manor house, but it doesn't look like a typical layout for a medieval manor house. There is a rectangular arrangement of walls around what looks as though it could be a courtyard surrounded by a range of cloisters. This of course means that the main building may not be a manor house at all but could be some kind of religious community building. This is one of the mysteries you are being asked to solve.'

Meanwhile, Josh was busy setting up the laptop ready to load up the flash drive containing the research data. He soon located the file containing the aerial photo. Meera pointed out that there were several interesting features showing up in the form of crop marks.

'Well, the perimeter of the courtyard is clearly visible, as is the outline of the main building, but as you can see, there is an interesting lighter area within the rectangle. Let's take a look at the geophysics – can you load it up Josh?'

'Sure thing Meera,' he replied, quickly locating the relevant file.

The picture that appeared on screen wasn't easy to read to the uninitiated, but fortunately the findings had been set down in the accompanying report which Meera began to summarise.

'Well pretty much as we might have expected, the main area of disturbance is showing up the shape of a large building. The anomalies created by the structure of the cloisters around the courtyard also show up well. The report goes on to confirm that, as we saw on the aerial photos, there is a smaller area of interest, showing some soil disturbance, in the courtyard area. At this stage we aren't aware that the burial ground extended beyond the northern boundary so it's possible that if this is a burial, it may be much older than the building itself, or it could be some kind of natural anomaly.'

Meera then explained how they were to proceed. Initially, they were to clear the turf and topsoil from three rectangular areas, each approximately fifteen feet square, and then excavate any interesting features which showed up within them.

Turning to the students, she asked them,

'Where would you suggest we should place the initial excavation areas?'

After a short silence, a couple of hands went up.

'Yes Marcia?' Meera queried,

'Perhaps one could be across the corner of the main building, where it meets the cloister wall?'

'Yes, that's a good suggestion. What were you thinking Colin?'

'Well, definitely one across one side of the cloister walls, I should think.'

'That makes sense,' Meera agreed, then went on, 'OK, one more then. Anyone?'

After a few moments pause, a young woman standing to one side of the group put up her hand and when Meera nodded in her direction, spoke softly, saying,

'What about placing one inside the courtyard, over the smaller crop mark?'

'Perfect Samira,' Meera replied, 'OK let's get them marked out.'

She divided the students into three groups and allocated each group to one of the Field Assistant Supervisors. Celine was to work on the area across the building, Josh would supervise the excavation across the cloister and Pete was to deal with the one inside the courtyard.

After the teams had marked out the position of the area they were to investigate, Meera suggested they all take an early lunch break before starting to dig. She was glad the weather was holding. The forecast had been mixed, but thankfully there was still no sign of rain. After half an hour, eager to make a start, they picked up their gear and headed out into the field.

Meera watched as Adam and Samira, the students working with Pete, prepared to remove the turf layer from the trench. As Adam sunk his spade into the ground, Meera suddenly felt a distinct chill and shivered involuntarily. She glanced across at Samira who was standing next to Adam, and muttered,

'Goodness, it's turning colder all at once. Perhaps it's blowing for rain after all.'

Samira looked a little puzzled but began to dig alongside Adam.

Meera returned to the tent to take a further look at the research information to make sure they hadn't missed anything important in their assessment of the site and if so, how it would be best to tackle it. Her mind returned once more to her father, as it had been doing frequently as she had been planning this project. Inevitably her thoughts also went to her mother. She had always been closer to her father than to her mother and had often wondered why that was. Physically they were quite different. For one thing her mother tended to gain weight all too easily, whilst Meera herself was small and slim. Temperamentally also, they were poles apart. Her mother had spent her working life supporting her father, helping with his research and always content to bask in his successes, acting more as a secretary than a colleague or even a wife. Meera couldn't understand why she had so little ambition in her own right.

As she thought about why she had been closer to her father, she concluded that their common interest in archaeology had probably strengthened the bond between the two of them. However, she had always felt her career had never quite lived up to his expectations, which had caused some tension between them in more recent times.

Meera decided she had left the students to it long enough and went outside to see what progress they had made. The turf had been removed, and they had now begun carefully excavating the soil using their trowels. For the next couple of hours, they continued to remove the layers of earth, and already Josh's team was beginning to uncover what looked like the remains of a wall. As Meera looked down into Pete's trench, he pointed out an area of soil which looked like infill from an earlier excavation, and he was eager to carry on digging, but when Meera glanced at her watch, she decided it was getting late. Digs usually finished at around four, and it was three forty-five already.

She called out across the site,

'OK everyone, let's call it a day and get cleaned up.'

It took them half an hour to clean and stash away the gear in the vehicles and tidy up the site. They were all staying in the vicinity for the duration of the dig and now drove down the lane to the village at the bottom of the hill.

Chapter 2

The students were staying in a barn at the edge of Little Stretford. It had been converted into a kind of youth hostel. There was a kitchen with communal cooking facilities. Pete, Celine, and Josh organised the four students who had volunteered to do the cooking that day and they began to prep the food. Asking them to have the meal ready for six thirty, Meera and her team left them to it.

They were staying at the Crooked Gate pub a hundred yards down the village road and they went off to check in, telling the students they would be back at six-fifteen to eat with them.

A typical English village pub, all beams, and low ceilings, it was warm and welcoming. The landlord was behind the bar and was obviously expecting them and greeted them warmly. After asking them to sign into the register he handed them each a room key and showed them the way up the back stairs to the bedrooms. They were small but comfortable, although to Meera's disappointment, without en-suite bathrooms.

It was now five o'clock and after they'd settled in and cleaned up, one by one, they drifted down to the bar. A couple of bearded, weather-beaten old locals were sitting at the table under the window playing dominoes. News always spread fast in the village, so of course, they already knew that the strangers had been up at the old church at the top of the hill all day.

'What you doin' up theer then?' one of them asked in a broad local accent.

Meera smiled and explained that they were a team of archaeologists who were conducting an excavation near the church.

The men glanced at one another, then the one who had already spoken went on,

'Well, you wants to be careful, you might dig up more than you bargained for. What do you say Bert?' he asked of his companion.

Grinning at his friend, Bert replied,

'Aye Tom, there's allus bin summat strange up theer in't ther?! I wouldn't want to be in their shoes, would you?'

'I'm sure we'll be fine, we're used to digging up old bones,' Josh piped up, 'unless there's something you want to tell us?'

'Nay, just you be careful that's all,' replied Tom, picking up the dominoes that Bert had just set down in front of him.

With that, the two old men went on with their game. Josh grinned at Pete and with a roll of his eyes, and slight shake of his head, indicated that they should just ignore them. Meera had never been of a nervous disposition when unearthing bones from burial sites, but for some reason what the old men had just said, suddenly made her feel uneasy. Telling herself not to be stupid, she stood up and went up to the bar to get herself a drink.

As she poured Meera's fruit juice, the landlady, who had heard the exchange, declared,

'You don't want to take any notice of those two.'

'Oh, I know! In our line of work, we're always coming across the odd local with strange tales to tell. I think sometimes people don't like the idea of us coming along stirring things up.'

'What are you hoping to find though?' the landlady went on.

'We're working on the field behind the church investigating the site of a medieval building.'

'That's interesting. Well, you're all booked in for six weeks, but how long do you think you'll be here?'

'We hope to finish by then, if all goes smoothly.'

Paying for her drink and thanking the landlady, Meera sat down with the others for half an hour or so before they all decided it was time to go along to the barn for supper.

The curry and rice went down well, the students had done a good job, and everyone seemed in a good mood and looking forward to getting stuck in the following morning. After supper Meera and the others left the students to it and made their way back to the pub for a nightcap, where they found Tom and Bert still engrossed in their dominoes.

Meera felt they were a friendly team by and large. She had worked with Josh and Celine in the past and knew them well. Josh was the joker in the pack. He was married with two children, a son fifteen and a daughter, twelve. He was a good sort, dependable even though he often didn't seem to take things seriously enough. Career-wise he wasn't particularly ambitious. He already had his MA but was content to leave it at that for now at least and wasn't going for a PhD.

Celine was studying for her masters' and was also a competent field assistant supervisor, hard-working and attentive. She rarely missed a clue and usually had a pretty accurate idea as to what it was indicating. Meera also knew Celine's wife Diana. They had been married for three years now and seemed very happy together. They were going through the lengthy process of adopting a child.

Pete Shore was single and as far as Meera knew, not in a long-term relationship. He was around her age, and pleasant enough. Like herself, he seemed wedded to his career. He never spoke much about his life outside of the job and archaeology. As Meera sat at the table, joining in the conversation, she was feeling that this was going to be a good dig. The students seemed to be gelling, as were her assistants. At this point she became aware the conversation had turned to the soil disturbance in Pete's excavated area,

'What d'you think's going on with that one Pete, is it a burial do you think?'

'I'm honestly not sure Josh. It looks like there's quite a lot of soil disturbance. Hopefully, tomorrow we'll be able to find out.'

Tom and Bert, who were still playing dominoes, were also listening in, and suddenly Bert called out,

'Well, don't forget. Just you be careful!'

'Ee's right. There's somethin' strange up theer. Don't say we didn't warn you,' Tom agreed.

'Well thanks for the warning gentlemen, we'll keep an eye out!' Josh called across the room, winking and smiling at Meera, who smiled back. However, once again she felt that chill in the air, even though the pub was warm, and the windows were shut tight.

'Well, we've got an early start tomorrow. I want to be up at the site by eight. We're having breakfast here at seven, so I'm off to bed, and I suggest we all call it a night.'

'Sure thing boss, I'm ready myself,' Josh replied with a mock salute, and one by one, they stood up to leave, calling across to Tom and Bert to say goodnight.

'Night all!' Tom replied, then couldn't resist grinning at Bert before adding, 'Think on now!'

It took Meera a long time to fall asleep. She struggled in vain to quieten her mind which was ranging between wondering what they would find the next day and how it would relate to her father's report, Tom and

Bert's disturbing warnings, and the characters of the various students and what she would need to do to help them get the best out of the project. Eventually she fell asleep but spent a restless night which she put down to being in a strange bed.

The buzzing of the alarm on her phone dragged her from the only decent hour of sleep she'd managed throughout the night. Wearily reaching across, she grabbed it and turned off the alarm. She was soon in the bathroom, eager to get there before anyone else. While showering, she was thinking of the day ahead, thankful that at least the weather looked good again. Digging could be hard enough in the sunshine, but especially so in the pouring rain. Once again, she shivered, despite the hot water pouring down her back. Trying to ignore these troubling sensations, she quickly got out of the shower and dried herself before putting on her robe and padding towards her room, passing Celine, looking tousled, and heading in the opposite direction.

'Morning,' Meera said, smiling, 'did you sleep well?'

'Not really,' Celine replied, 'a strange bed, I guess.'

'I know what you mean,' Meera went on, 'probably be better tonight.'

Meera rummaged in her case and found clean undies and top. Pulling on her 'digging-jeans' and trainers, she brushed her hair, tying it back in a ponytail, and after taking a quick glance in the mirror was ready for the day. She made her way down to the bar, which doubled as a dining room, and was surprised to see that Josh was already there and helping himself to cereal from the serving table at the end of the room.

'Mornin!' he called over to Meera as she came in.

'Crikey, it's not like you to be first up!' she quipped.

'Well, you did send us to bed early, I'm not used to being told when it's my bedtime!' Josh said, smiling broadly, 'I did get a good sleep though, what about you?'

'Don't ask,' she replied as she helped herself to a cup of tea and a bowl of muesli.

'Probably the weight of the responsibility of organising us lot, preying on your mind!'

'Something like that,' Meera responded, smiling.

Sitting down together at a table under the window they chatted amiably until the others appeared. They seemed bright and ready to get stuck into a day's digging. After helping themselves to breakfast they chatted for a while before Meera stood up, saying,

'Right, are we ready? We've got a fine day for it, so let's get moving.'

Chapter 3

After calling in at the village store to pick up sand-wiches for their lunch, they collected the students from the barn. They all piled into the vehicles, and it was just after eight fifteen as they turned in through the gate leading up to the church. The air was chill, the mist still in the meadows and lingering around the ruins.

When preparing the proposal for this project, Meera had carried out her usual online searches and had been shocked but rather bemused to find that there had indeed been many rumours over the years, of strange occurrences at Old Saint Paul's. Not having the slightest interest in such things, believing them to be the imaginings of self-indulgent sorts who liked nothing better than frightening vulnerable people, she had dismissed them from her mind. However, glancing up at the church now with swirls of mist hanging around its ruined walls, together with the old timers' comments the night before, she could half believe it. If ever there was a spooky place to be digging up stuff, this must be it, she thought.

An hour later, the students were hard at work carefully removing layer after layer of earth. Josh and his team were now brushing the soil away from the masonry, gradually exposing more of a possible wall, or a foundation of the cloister, they had glimpsed the day before. Celine's team were in their trench, still scraping with their trowels. They had also discovered the remains of a wall, or rather the point where two walls met at right angles.

Having removed another couple of layers of soil, Pete was more convinced than ever that he was dealing with a burial site of some kind and suggested to Meera that they now concentrate on excavating the area with the looser soil deposit. Meera agreed and Pete and a couple of the students began working solely on that area, while the rest of his team carried on removing soil layers from the rest of their trench.

Nothing much else turned up for the rest of the day. By three o'clock Pete and his team had excavated down to around three feet, but so far hadn't reached any archaeological features. Then, just as they were about to pack up for the day, Samira called out,

'Over here! I think I've found something!'

Pete stepped over to where Samira was working, scrutinising the ground in front of her. Meera had hurried across and, as is the custom, after asking Pete if it was okay for her to enter the trench, jumped down to see what Samira had discovered. She was scraping with her trowel, exposing what looked like the remains of a fabric object.

'What do you think, Meera?' he asked.

Meera replied, 'It looks like the remains of a blanket of some kind, but it doesn't look ancient to me, more like a car rug or similar.'

'That's what I thought,' Pete said thoughtfully.

Picking up a brush from the finds tray at the side of the trench, he knelt down and as he began carefully brushing the soil away, a cold wind suddenly blew across the soil, as if assisting him.

'Where did that come from?' Meera asked of no-one in particular. She watched Pete painstakingly removing the soil from the fabric, wondering if there could be something wrapped up in it.

That's odd, Meera thought. She had seen no mention of this in her father's report on the site, but it seemed incredible that he could have missed it, unless it had been placed here after his excavations. Well, having found it, they would have to carefully remove the remnants of the blanket tomorrow to find out whether it was covering anything else. For tonight though, they could leave it undisturbed.

'OK everyone, let's call it a day,' she called out to the others.

After tidying up the site and covering the trenches with tarpaulins, they packed their gear before heading back down to the village, and possibly another restless night for Meera. She had plenty to think about.

Why had her father not included this in his report? And why was the blanket buried in the earth three feet below the surface? Add to that the several strange sensations she'd been experiencing since arriving in this village, and it was developing as a mystery she was determined to solve.

That evening after supper there was much discussion about the finds of the day. Josh was sure his team had discovered the foundations of the cloister walls. Celine's team were now certain they had found the corner of the main building along with pieces of pottery which would provide important dating evidence.

Everyone though, was fascinated with Pete's team's discovery of the blanket, all speculating as to what, if anything had been wrapped up in it.

'Maybe it contains a body!' Josh exclaimed gleefully.

'Why would someone just wrap it in a blanket?' Celine asked of no one in particular.

'Maybe they needed to dispose of it quickly and didn't have a coffin to put the body in, so just wrapped it in a blanket to bury it!' Adam offered, smiling.

Meera felt this was all getting a bit silly, and said,

'We'll find out soon enough tomorrow. I'm off down to the pub, are you ready Josh?'

'Sure thing,' he replied, 'Pete, Celine?'

They decided to leave the vehicles at the barn and walk down to the pub as it was a fine moonlit night. As they turned out of the drive into the village street,

Meera glanced up towards the church and was stopped in her tracks as she thought she saw a light shining through one of the ruined windows.

'Josh,' she whispered, 'I'm sure there's someone up at the church, look!'

But by the time Josh had looked towards the top of the hill, there was no sign of a light of any kind.

'This place has got you spooked I reckon!' he said, 'I can't see anything. Maybe just a trick of the moonlight shining through the mist.'

'You're probably right,' Meera commented, but without conviction.

When they walked into the bar of the Crooked Gate, they weren't surprised to see the two old timers there again, playing their dominoes.

Tom looked up and grinning at Bert, called out,

'Evenin! Found anythin' interestin' yet?'

Meera smiled and said,

'Sorry gentlemen, nothing of interest I'm afraid.'

With that, the old men finished their game then got up to leave, wishing them all goodnight, but couldn't resist grinning at each other again as Tom called out,

'It be a full moon tha' knows, so ye must tek extra care!'

Meera just nodded and smiled at them as they left. After getting a drink from the bar they all sat down now in one of the alcoves to recap the day's events. Meera was keen to find out how they thought the students were getting on and whether she needed to have a word with any of them. They all confirmed that they seemed a bright enough bunch and there were no major issues. Then the conversation inevitably turned to the business of the blanket.'.

'That's damned odd, you know,' Josh offered. 'Why would a car blanket, which can't be that old, be buried three feet down?'

'I know,' Meera replied. 'It is strange.'

'What did the report of the previous excavation say about it, Meera?' Pete asked, 'I believe it was one of your father's projects, wasn't it?'

Meera hesitated slightly before answering,

'It was, Pete. That's just the thing though. His report doesn't mention finding anything of the sort.'

'What! How can that be? Surely anyone excavating that site would have discovered and commented on such an unusual find.'

Meera didn't like the way this conversation was going, and desperate to find another explanation, said quickly,

'Well, I suppose it's possible it wasn't there at the time but has been placed there since. My father's project was carried out years ago, so it's likely that it was buried more recently, less than thirty-five years ago in fact.'

'Curiouser and curiouser!' Josh declared, and standing up, asked, 'Anyone fancy another one?'

They chatted on for another hour before Celine announced she was off to bed, and Meera said she was ready to go too. Josh and Pete said they'd have another drink before turning in, so the women left them to it.

It was well after midnight by the time Meera had fallen into a fitful sleep. She had eventually drifted off thinking about the blanket in the trench. What had been buried in it? Could it be human remains, or in fact, only an old blanket, which would have been odd in itself.

As her waking mind shut down, her thoughts transformed themselves into a vivid dream. She was standing alone gazing down into the trench, when suddenly the soil around the remains of the blanket in the bottom began to move. Oddly, she didn't feel afraid, just curious. As she watched, first a skeletal hand pushed its way out, followed by another. To her horror the disembodied hands started reaching up towards her as if trying to grab hold of her. She screamed 'No!' then suddenly found herself awake, trembling and sweating with fear.

There was a gentle knocking on the door, and she heard Celine whisper,

'Are you alright Meera?'

'Oh, yes, sorry, did I wake you? It was just a bad dream.'

'No problem, as long as you're ok. Goodnight.'

'Goodnight!' Meera called out, feeling utterly foolish.

She had never been prone to having nightmares, in fact she couldn't remember ever having had one at all. So, she wondered, what on earth was that all about? It took her a good hour to calm down enough to get off to sleep again, but this time, thankfully without any further visitations.

Chapter 4

Alex could hear the waves gently lapping on the shore and the seagulls wheeling overhead as she dozed in the deckchair. She was feeling more relaxed than she'd done for weeks, months, in fact. It had been a good decision to take a week off and come down to Tidmouth with Dave and the kids.

Her last case had been particularly harrowing, involving a child abduction. It had ended in a dreadful tragedy, but thankfully, the child had finally been returned to his father. It had taken a lot out of Alex emotionally, and Dave, wise as ever, suggested they all needed a break. The obvious choice was to come down to Tidmouth to spend some time with her parents, Ted, and Dorothy.

Johnny and Aby were always happy to be here, with their grandparents, and Alex in particular needed to spend time with her mother who had been fighting bowel cancer for months. Having undergone surgery followed by chemo, it seemed that she was over the worst and would hopefully only need regular checkups in the future.

Holding down such a demanding job had meant Alex had been unable to be as supportive as she would have liked. Not that her mum ever complained. It had, she feared, put a huge strain on Ted though. The worry, constant hospital visits and inevitably having to do much more around the house had definitely taken its toll. He seemed to have aged ten years since her mum's diagnosis a year or so ago.

Dave and Ted had taken Johnny and Aby fossil hunting along the beach, something the kids had never tired of doing. However, Alex was only too aware things may change before long. Johnny would soon be off to study Computer Science in Manchester and the way these things often went, he may never again return home permanently. Their tight-knit little family of four may soon become three for a while. Aby would be with them for some time yet though.

More often than not, they had visited Tidmouth just for a weekend, so it had been lovely to spend these leisurely days with her mum and dad. Back home tomorrow though, she mused. I wonder what's been going on there while I've been away. Being a Detective Inspector, one of the good things about her job was that she never knew from day to day what was going to turn up.

Alex opened her eyes now and turned to look at her mum in the deckchair beside her. She was snoring softly. Alex was so grateful that she'd come through the last few months. When Dorothy had first told her that it was 'the Big C' as she put it, Alex had been worried sick that she was going to lose her. An only child, she had always been particularly close to her mother. Now, it seemed, they would have many more years of memories to make together.

As she glanced along the beach she could see Dave, Ted and the kids making their way along the shoreline. Gently touching her mother's arm to rouse her, she said,

'Our peace is about to be shattered mum; the fossil hunters are back!'

Dorothy sleepily opened her eyes and asked what the time was.

'About four Mum.' Alex replied.'

'Good heavens, it's time we got back, I've got a roast to put in for supper!'

'Don't worry Mum, we'll soon get it sorted. There's no rush anyway, it will be just perfect to have a relaxing dinner on our last night here.'

'Well, it's been lovely having you all here.'

'All the same, I bet you'll enjoy the peace when we've gone,' Alex replied, smiling.

'To be honest, I can have too much peace. The more the merrier for me,' Dorothy went on, then added with a grin, 'but of course, I can't speak for your dad.'

Alex had begun to pack up the remnants of their day as the others arrived.

'Anything left to eat Mum?' Johnny asked hopefully.

'Here you go,' Alex replied, holding out a box containing a couple of tuna sandwiches, 'Just one each left.'

'Thanks,' Johnny said as he eagerly grabbed the box.

Aby, who had been lagging behind had just turned up, shouting,

'Hey! I want one too!'

'I know, don't panic, little sister,' Johnny responded in a patronising tone, as Aby snatched the sandwich he was offering.

'Manners!' he exclaimed, as she slumped down on the sand beside her grandma to eat her sandwich.

'Honestly, you two!' Dorothy exclaimed, 'It's time you stopped bickering like this.'

'Sorry Grandma,' Johnny replied, 'but she's soo annoying!'

At this point Dave exclaimed,

'For goodness sake Johnny! Give it a rest! Anyway, come on now and give me a hand to get this lot back to the car.'

Later that evening as they lay in bed, Alex and Dave were mulling over the last few days.

'It's been great to spend some quality time with your Mum and Dad love,' Dave began, 'nothing's ever too much trouble for them, is it? Ted really enjoyed today fossil hunting with the kids.'

'I know love, and it was so nice to spend a quiet hour or two on the beach with Mum. She seems so much better. She's got this check-up the day after tomorrow, but it's just routine.'

'Yes, Ted mentioned it. It's such a relief to know it's apparently under control love,' Dave replied.

'It is. I really thought at one point that we might lose her, but now it looks like she'll be with us for many more years yet.'

'Well, home tomorrow. I want to get away fairly early, if that's ok with you.'

'Absolutely,' Alex replied, 'I'm beginning to wonder what's been going on at the station while I've been away, so I'd like to be home by early afternoon.'

'Well goodnight love,' Dave said softly as they turned over and were soon asleep.

In fact, it was eleven-thirty by the time they were ready to leave the next day, after Dorothy had insisted on cooking them a 'full English', which pleased Johnny and Aby. They were always ready for one of 'Grandma's breakfasts' as they called any plate of bacon and eggs they came across.

After they'd packed the car there were hugs all round.

'Thanks for coming down,' Ted said to Dave as they shook hands.

Alex hugged her mum saying.

'Let me know how your check-up goes. Look after yourself Mum.'

'I will, and you too! Don't work too hard.'

Alex smiled,

'Can't promise that Mum.'

Then they were in the car and watching Ted and Dorothy standing at the gate smiling and waving. As she waved back to them Alex promised to herself that she would definitely try to come more often. The cancer scare had reminded her how fragile life is, and that they wouldn't be around forever.

After being held up in traffic for a good half hour, it was almost two by the time they turned into the drive. After unpacking the car, Alex lost no time in ringing Sally Nugent, her sergeant,

'Hi Sally, we just got home. Anything much happened while I've been away?'

'Hi Boss. Well, it's been quiet here. Just the usual stuff really. Nothing we couldn't handle. I'll fill you in when you get back in.'

'Well, I'll be in tomorrow morning bright and early, ready to tackle whatever the criminal fraternity decide to throw at us.'

'That's good to hear Boss. See you in the morning then.'

Alex spent the rest of the day unpacking, washing the holiday clothes and getting the school uniforms ready for Johnny and Aby. Dave offered to cook supper and served up a presentable tuna pasta bake. The youngsters escaped to their rooms afterwards to catch up with their gaming, and Alex and Dave opened a bottle of Beaujolais and relaxed with their favourite playlist for an hour or two.

'I wonder what tomorrow will bring,' Alex pondered aloud.

'Well, I hope it won't be as stressful for you as the last case,' Dave responded.

'Oh, I don't know, I think I'm ready for another challenge,' Alex announced with a grin, blissfully unaware of what lay ahead.

Chapter 5

As they were eating breakfast the next morning, Meera apologised to Celine.

'I'm sorry if I woke you up last night Celine, I just had a bit of a nightmare.'

'I told you this place has got you spooked,' Josh said, grinning.

'Well, something must have for sure,' Meera replied, 'That damned blanket and what it might contain certainly figured prominently anyway!'

'Well, today the mystery will be solved,' Pete said with conviction.

After breakfast they walked along to the barn to collect the vehicles and found the students raring to go.

They're certainly a keen lot, Meera thought to herself, but then there's nothing like a mystery to spark some enthusiasm. They all piled into the vehicles and made their way up the track to the church.

'Right, let's get to it,' Meera encouraged.

Collecting their gear from the tent, they trouped out onto the site. Meera made straight for Pete's trench but as she approached, was annoyed to see that one of the corners of the tarpaulin was turned back.

'Pete, are you sure you secured the tarpaulin last night?'

'You know I did Meera; you saw me place that stone on the corner, just like I did on all of them. How it got moved I've no idea.'

'Well let's have a look, I hope no-one's been messing around up here. I told you I thought I saw a light, didn't I?'

Pete pulled back the tarpaulin, and they all peered down into the trench, but couldn't see anything amiss.

'Just another spooky occurrence then,' Josh joked, but Meera didn't find that in the least bit amusing.

At the dig it took them a couple of hours' work to carefully remove the rest of the soil covering the blanket. Looking at its shape, Meera and Pete glanced knowingly at each other. It was obvious to them both that human remains may well be about to emerge. Suddenly, Adam called out,

'Here, I've found something!'

Meera jumped down into the trench and stood close by, carefully observing what was slowly being exposed as he pulled the blanket aside.

'It certainly looks as though we have a body!' she announced,

Pete gasped aloud and when Meera looked at him, she could see he had turned ashen. Maybe this is his first body, she thought, then turned to Adam, who contrary to Meera's expectations, looked excited at the prospect of excavating his first one.

'This is undoubtedly the ribs,' Meera confirmed.

As Adam continued to remove the blanket from around the bones, at one end of the line of ribs, the skull began to emerge. At that moment, an overpowering feeling of grief swept over Meera. Although she often felt a certain empathy for the person who had once lived, she'd never experienced this level of emotion before when excavating a burial. This was different. When she glanced around to speak to Pete, he was no longer in the trench. Meera looked questioningly at Belinda, who indicated that he had walked off toward the finds tent.

As Meera clambered out of the trench. Josh was standing, gazing down at the exposed bones.

'That's a turn up and no mistake!' he exclaimed.

Still feeling emotional, Meera started to answer him but to her horror, her voice trembled a little as she said quietly,

'I know Josh, it's all very odd. How come a body wrapped in a relatively modern blanket would have been buried without ceremony three feet beneath the surface.'

With that, she called out to the rest of the team that it was time to take a break and headed for the church. One by one they put down their trowels and climbed out of their trenches to follow Josh, Adam, and Meera to the tent. Celine couldn't resist pausing to take a look at what had been found. As she gazed down, she noticed something glinting in the soil close to one side of the skull. As this wasn't her trench, she resisted stepping in to take a closer look, just making a mental note to mention it to Meera.

Pete was sitting on one of the folding chairs, still not looking too good, when Meera entered the tent.

'You alright?' Meera asked him.

'Yeah, I'm fine Meera. It was just more of a shock than I'd expected. I'm sorry I walked off the job, I just needed a minute.'

'No problem,' Meera reassured him, 'to be honest, seeing that it's been apparently wrapped in a blanket and thrown into a hole in the ground shocked me too. No one should be laid to rest like that, particularly as we think it's a fairly recent burial.'

Samira, who had been standing beside her listening to the exchange, asked,

'What if it isn't a proper burial at all?'

'I know what you're suggesting Samira, and of course, we will have to notify the police. Unfortunately, that will mean shutting down the trench, and maybe the whole site. I need to be sure what we're dealing with first.'

'Oh, of course!' Samira replied quickly.

'Shall I make a brew, boss?' Belinda called out.

'Thanks Belinda. That sounds great.'

Ten minutes later they were all sitting down enjoying their tea, when Celine decided now was a good time to mention what she'd noticed in the trench.

'I don't know whether you saw it,' she said, 'but there's a small shiny object to the left-hand side of the skull. I didn't get down to look more closely of course, but it looks like gold, as though it could be a piece of jewellery.'

'No, I didn't see that, we'll take a look when we go out, thanks Celine,' Meera replied, cursing herself for missing it. She must, she concluded, have been distracted by the emotional response she'd had to the discovery of the body. A find in the vicinity of the body could provide important dating evidence.

They spent twenty minutes or so discussing the possible significance of this rather strange burial, and also what had been found in the other trenches. Josh was now convinced that what his team had unearthed was the foundation of a cloister, indicating that the building was indeed a religious one of some kind.

Meera finally said it was time to get back to digging, and they all trouped out to pick up where they'd left off. She was eager to locate the item Celine had spotted and immediately found it peeping out of the soil near the top of the spine, just a few inches to the left of the skull. Samira was looking at it intently and was the first to exclaim,

'It's an earring!!'

The significance of the earring wasn't lost on any of them. The body had obviously been wrapped in the blanket, with no sign of the remains of a coffin, and with what looked like a modern earring lying beside the skull, indicating that it had been deposited relatively recently. Within thirty years, Meera estimated from the condition of the skeleton. Also, the fact it was not lying on an east to west alignment meant this person hadn't had a christian burial. Everything was now pointing to this being a crime scene.

Meera knew that all work would have to be stopped, and the police informed that what appeared to be relatively recently buried human remains had been located. If they concluded that it was a suspicious burial, they would notify the coroner. Once it was in the coroner's hands there may be a delay before they were allowed to continue with that particular trench. She hoped they would be able to carry on excavating the rest of the site, but that would be the coroner's decision. If the body turned out to be recent, the investigation would be a criminal one managed by the police, aided by their forensic team.

'OK everyone, we have to stop all work until the police have taken a look.'

There was a collective moan as she spoke, even though they had all known what was coming. They understood it was essential to call in the police if unexpected human remains were found.

Meera asked Josh to photograph all the trenches, with close ups of the skull and earring in situ. She also asked Pete to make a sketch of the burial, accurately recording the position of the skeleton. While the team were gathering up their equipment, Meera went back to the tent to call the police.

Chapter 6

After speaking briefly with a couple of people, explaining the reason for her call, and being held on the line for several minutes, Meera was finally put through to one of the detectives,

Alex was at her desk, catching up with paperwork when her phone rang. Picking it up she answered with her usual,

'Good afternoon, DI Alex Scott here. How can I help?'

'Good morning,' Meera replied, 'I'm Dr Meera Carter, archaeologist, and I'm heading up a project excavating land adjacent to Old Saint Paul's church, Little Stretford. Are you familiar with it?'

'I am. What is the problem?' Alex responded, thinking that this sounded interesting.

'I'm reporting the discovery of human remains deposited in an unusual situation, which in itself is suspicious, but also it's wrapped in a blanket or car rug.'

Now Meera had Alex's full attention.

'OK, I'll organise a team to secure the site and will be over this afternoon with the paperwork. Meanwhile I'm assuming you have suspended all activity there?'

'I have, of course,' Meera replied.

'Good, and please make sure that no one enters the site at all. I have your number on-screen, so I'll text mine across to you, in case you need to contact me.'

'Thank you. Any idea what time you might be able to come?'

'I should be with you by two o'clock. See you later Dr Carter.'

'Thank you, I'll look forward to it.'

Meera glanced up to find that her team were just entering the tent and explained,

'I've just informed the police. Hopefully, a DI Scott will be here at two o'clock to make her assessment. Meanwhile she's sending a team to secure the site. I don't yet know whether the coroner will allow us to carry on excavating the rest of the site. Until we know one way or the other, we'll just have to wait. We may as well get some lunch now; we can't do anything more here until the police arrive.'

It was about an hour later when a car turned up and three uniformed officers strode into the tent. One was obviously a sergeant. He was accompanied by two young constables carrying metal posts and rolls of hazard tape. The sergeant asked for Dr Carter, and Meera stood up, saying,

'Good afternoon. I expect you're here to secure the site?'

'Sergeant Shapiro, ma'am. Yes, DI Scott has asked us to cordon it off, pending further investigations. I'd be grateful if you would show us where the remains are.'

'Of course,' Meera replied, 'I have an old map here showing the area we are meant to be excavating,'

The sergeant went over to look at the map and Meera pointed out the extent of the site, and the position of Pete's trench.

'Do you mind if I borrow this while we mark out the area?'

'Not at all, please take it, but I will need it back when you've finished.'

'Thanks,' the sergeant nodded, then turning to the two young constables, he went on, 'This way you two.'

Within half an hour they had placed hazard tape right around the whole of the site, with 'no entry' signs on each side and then 'stood guard' over it, which seemed a bit unnecessary to Meera.

As Alex Scott sat beside DC Neil Cotton, heading towards Little Stretford, she was thinking to herself that this case seemed as though it would be an interesting one. A body buried in suspicious circumstances, maybe some years earlier, would present her with some new challenges. She hadn't been involved in too many 'cold cases' which would probably require rather different approaches to the usual crimes she'd previously investigated. Also, the fact that it involved an archaeological investigation was interesting. It was something she'd not had much experience of. However, always eager to learn, she was looking forward to understanding the finer points of dealing with the particular challenges it may present.

They arrived at the site on the dot of two. Having scanned the occupants of the tent she had successfully identified that Meera was in charge, and now approached her with outstretched hand saying,

'Detective Inspector Alex Scott. You are Dr Carter, I presume?'

'Yes, I am, Meera Carter. Would you like to take a look at the site first?' she responded.

'Yes, thanks, I need to get an idea what we might be dealing with here,' Alex replied.

Pete, who had anticipated that the tarpaulin would need to be removed for the DI to inspect the grave, had already donned protective shoe coverings and gloves and followed them out of the tent.

They surveyed the site and without stepping inside the tapes, Meera pointed out the burial trench, covered with the tarpaulin sheet for now. However, she was shocked to see that once again, one corner of the tarpaulin was thrown back. That's odd, she thought. She knew Pete had been careful to cover the whole trench before they walked off the site. Could it have been blown off by the wind? But there was no wind! As she was processing this in her mind DI Scott, who obviously missed nothing, asked in a concerned voice,

'Why has that corner been turned back? The last thing we need is some animal or other getting in there before forensics have done their work.'

Annoyed by Alex's rather officious tone which had placed her on the defensive, Meera declared brusquely,

'I have no idea how that can have happened. My team were careful to cover the trench securely,' she said, glancing meaningfully at Pete, who had stepped over the tapes and was now removing the tarpaulin from the trench.

Alex peered down into the grave. Meera pointed to the skull and then the earring,

'As it's lying adjacent to the skull, it looks likely that the occupant had been wearing it when they died. The body had been wrapped in what looks like a car rug which indicates that it was buried relatively recently. Also the alignment of the body isn't east to west, as would be the case with a usual Christian burial.'

'Thankyou Dr Carter. In that case everything does seem to indicate that it is a suspicious burial, and I need to close the site down immediately and inform the coroner.'

'Of course,' Meera replied rather testily.

'I've brought the paperwork with me, if you wouldn't mind completing it for me?'

Meera instructed Pete to secure the tarpaulin over the trench once more.

'Make sure it's secure this time Pete,' she added pointedly.

Pete looked as if he was about to speak, then thought better of it.

As they returned to the tent, Alex asked Meera to read through a couple of forms she'd brought with her, stating that she was taking over the site temporarily until the remains and anything else suspicious which may be found, had been thoroughly investigated.

Pete was sure he had covered the trench carefully before, but this time, to make certain, he placed a couple of heavy stones across the corner of the tarpaulin. That should do it, he thought, nothing'll get in, or out for that matter, now. As he walked away, a sudden blast of cold air once again blew across the site and the hairs on the back of his neck stood up as he hurried back into the tent.

Alex was thanking Meera for her help and left shortly afterwards, saying she'd be in touch when she'd spoken to the coroner. As Meera watched her leave, she was thinking that Alex Scott seemed rather full of herself, but then, she supposed, it was all part of her job.

As for Alex, she was thinking that Dr Meera Carter seemed like a bit of a prickly customer. Not used to having her professionalism challenged, Alex thought, she might need more careful handling as she may need her cooperation and expertise in the future.

Chapter 7

Arriving at the station Alex immediately rang the coroner's office. She was put through to Mr Grainger, the Deputy Coroner.

'Hello, Arthur Grainger here. How can I help?'

'Ah! Mr Grainger, it's DI Alex Scott here. I'm ringing to request a visit to an archaeological dig at Little Stretford, next to Old St Paul's. Do you know it?'

'Hello DI Scott. No, I've not had any dealings with that area before. What have they found?'

'They've found human remains.'

'I see, was this unexpected?'

'It was,' Alex replied, 'and the circumstances of the burial were also odd, as you will see for yourself.'

'Okay, I'll try to get over there first thing in the morning,' Mr Grainger assured her.

'Thanks. The project manager is Dr Meera Carter. We have of course cordoned off the site and already informed her that no one must enter it for the moment. Perhaps you could let her know when you'll be arriving to make sure she's on site to speak to you. I'll text you her mobile number.'

'Thanks. I will of course let you know how we decide to proceed.'

After she'd put the phone down, Alex motioned to Neil who was sitting at his desk just outside her office, beckoning him to come in.

'Neil, we don't know much about this body yet, but we could start by looking at misspers in that area over the last forty years. Perhaps Mark could spend some time on that? Could you ask him to come in?'

'Sure Boss, I'll go get him.'

A few minutes later, Mark Jones knocked on the office door and Alex gestured for him to come in and sit down. After spending some minutes putting him in the picture, she asked if he could go back through the records of the last forty years, to find out if there were any unsolved disappearances within, say, twenty miles of Little Stretford.

Always keen to be given some real detective work, Mark eagerly agreed. He'd recently completed his probationary period after finishing his National Detective Program twelve months earlier and was keen to make his mark.

'Create a list of possibles. So far, we aren't sure of much about the remains, except that we believe they were deposited around thirty to forty years ago. Once the DNA and other tests are carried out, we'll be able to narrow the list down considerably.'

'Yes, of course Boss. I'll get on to it right away.'

'Thanks Mark,' Alex said with a smile. It was always good to have newly qualified people around, they're always so full of enthusiasm she thought, as she watched him hurry off to make a start on the task she'd given him.

The phone on Alex's desk rang. It was PC Dodds, down at the reception desk.

'What can I do for you PC Dodds?'

'I've got your husband here Ma'am,' he replied, 'Asking if he can see you.'

'He's here now?!' Alex exclaimed. She was concerned, he never came to the station. She immediately thought there must be something wrong.

'Of course, I'll be down right away,' she told him. Grabbing her jacket and bag she headed towards the lift, stopping only to explain to Neil where she was going.

As she stepped out into reception, Dave, who had been sitting in the waiting area stood up quickly and came towards her. She could tell immediately that he was not bringing good news.

'Oh love,' he said softly, 'can we go somewhere private?'

'What's happened Dave? Is it Johnny or Aby?' Alex asked, with rising panic in her voice.

Dave shook his head and looked pleadingly at her.

'Please Alex, let's go somewhere we can talk.'

With a feeling of dread welling up, Alex led him into a side room then again demanded what was wrong.

'Oh Alex, I'm so sorry.'

'Dave! For God's sake, tell me what's happened!' she almost shouted.

'It's your mum and dad,' he said softly.

'What do you mean, it's my mum and dad? Has there been an accident or something? I knew he was getting past driving!'

'Oh love, they're both dead.'

No, Alex thought, he must mean mum. Her mother had been fighting bowel cancer for some time and had seemed to be doing ok. No, he must mean mum, it can't be both of them!

After a moment's hesitation, trying to make sense of what he'd said, she replied,

'You mean mum! Oh Dave, and she'd been doing so well.'

'Alex, love, it's not just your mum, it's your dad too.'

Alex dropped down into a chair, completely unable to take it in.

'How? Why? What happened?' she managed, trying to steady her emotions while still not quite believing it.

'An accident love. It appears they were driving back home from the hospital appointment, and there was some kind of collision. The police turned up at home to let us know, but they didn't give many details. I expect they're still investigating. All we know for certain is that they both died at the scene.'

'Oh God Dave.'

As she spoke, the reality that her mum and dad were both gone. Impossible! She'd only said goodbye to them yesterday! The reality suddenly hit her and she crumpled. Shaking with emotion she fell into Dave's arms, and he held her tight without speaking, and just gave her time to try to compose herself. He knew that this wasn't the place for her to let go.

When she seemed calmer, he said,

'Come on love, let's get you home.'

'Dave, I can't, I'm in the middle of a case.'

'Yes you can, Alex. I'll contact Neil and explain what's happening and that you'll ring him later.'

Without further argument Alex followed him out to the car. Nothing seemed real. It all felt like a dream, or a nightmare to be more precise. Dave stood outside the car for a few minutes, on the phone to someone and Alex assumed it was probably Neil. He'd be putting him in the picture. Well, he and her sergeant, Sally, would have to step up for a while, she thought, until she could think straight and figure out what to do next, because as of this moment, she had no idea where to start. Her brain seemed to have seized up, utterly unable to process what Dave had just told her.

Dave got in and reached across, gripping her hand.

'Come on love, let's get home.'

The mention of home brought the children to mind.

'Oh good grief, Dave! The kids are going to be devastated. How will I be able to tell them? I don't think I can!'

'Don't worry love, I'll deal with that.'

Chapter 8

They drove home in silence, each with their own thoughts. Alex was still in a state of shock and disbelief, but as she tried to make sense of it, the questions had started to form in her mind. Dave felt it better to let her sit quietly to allow her to begin to process what had happened. He understood his wife well after twenty years of marriage. Her analytical brain would first and foremost want answers. What, where and when had it happened? Had they suffered or was the end instant? She would be ordering these thoughts as she sat beside him. Emotion would come later. There would be too many practical demands over the next days for her to give way to that yet. Not least of those was telling the children.

Ted and Dorothy had doted on Johnny and Aby. Alex being an only child, they were their only grandchildren, and they had spoiled them unashamedly. Living on the coast in Tidmouth helped of course. The family had spent many glorious weeks over the yearsr staying with them. Apart from Arnold, their dog, who had died a couple of years ago, this would be the first bereavement the children had experienced. They would need plenty of support and understanding to come to terms with it.

As Dave turned into the drive in front of 15 Wavertree Avenue, this thought was uppermost in Alex's mind. Dave had said he would tell them, but Alex decided at that moment that it had to be her, or at least, both of them together. She knew they should be home from school by now, probably each in their own rooms on their computers. Dave opened the door, and as Alex followed him in, she saw their coats hanging in the hall and their shoes scattered beneath, which confirmed it.

'Do you want me to go up to them?'

'No love, I need to be involved too,' Alex replied quietly.

'If you're sure, we can both do it. First, I'm going to make you a cup of tea with plenty of sugar in it, then when you're ready I'll go and ask them to come down.'

Ten minutes later Dave knocked first on Aby's then on Johnny's door, calling to them to come downstairs, as he and mum wanted to talk to them. Johnny, at sixteen, going on seventeed, was the eldest and his sister was two years younger. They bickered constantly but aside from the usual sibling rivalry, would defend each other staunchly in the face of a common enemy. When Aby had been experiencing bullying at school, it had been Johnny who had confronted her tormentor to put an end to it. Secretly she adored her big brother, but of course, would never tell him so.

Johnny arrived in the kitchen first, to find his parents looking rather formal, sitting at each end of the kitchen table.

'What's up?' he asked, rather concerned by their serious faces.

Dave answered, 'Let's wait for Aby, Johnny, there's something we need to tell you both together.'

They heard Aby bounding down the stairs and as she appeared at the door, she stopped abruptly seeing them all sitting at the table.

'What did you want to tell us? Mum?' she asked, looking Alex in the eye.

'Come and sit down, love,' Alex said gently.

'We have some very sad news for you both,' Dave said, glancing from one to the other of the children.

Johnny spoke first,

'What is it? Dad, you're scaring us. Is one of you ill?'

Aby, a little more perceptive than her brother and seeing how upset her mother looked, asked,

'Is it grandma?'

Alex's eyes filled with tears, but she managed to control her voice as she answered them,

'I'm so sorry, but there has been an accident. A serious one.'

'Are they hurt?' Johnny asked quickly.

Alex looked up at Dave and he could see she was finding it impossible to say the words. She nodded slightly, and he said softly,

'I'm so sorry you two, but I'm afraid neither of them made it.'

'What do you mean, they didn't make it?' Johnny asked.

Aby, however, was looking intently at her mother, who was struggling to contain her emotions. It was obvious to her that the unthinkable had happened.

'They're dead, aren't they?' she asked, her voice at that moment devoid of emotion. She understood that neither of her parents wanted to utter the words, so she had to.

Alex couldn't speak but just nodded her head. Johnny shouted,

'Nooo! They can't be! Dad?'

'It's true son,' Dave confirmed.

'But how, why, what happened,' Johnny asked, quietly now.

Aby was silent, but tears had now started to flow down her cheeks. She wasn't interested in how or why, only that they were gone. Those two people who had always been there, who had shown her nothing but love and kindness, were gone and were gone forever.

Dave went on to tell them what the police had said, which wasn't very much. Their grandad had been driving them home, apparently from a hospital appointment when there was a collision.

'Couldn't they save them?' Johnny asked, anger rising in his throat.

'No, they couldn't Johnny, apparently they both died instantly.'

With a wisdom far beyond her years, Aby observed through her tears,

'At least they both died together.'

At that point, Alex stood up and took her daughter in her arms and they clung together for mutual support.

Johnny sat, silent now, but from the set of his mouth Dave could see the anger he was fighting. He felt it too. Life could be such a bitch he thought. You can be jogging along one minute, then bang, everything changes in a moment, and you're left realising you aren't actually in control of your life after all!

Alex lay in bed that night, quite unable to sleep. She just couldn't accept that this was all really happening. She felt she needed to get down to Tidmouth. She needed to find out exactly what had happened, to visit the scene, to see her mum and dad, however difficult that was. Until she saw them, she wouldn't be convinced this was real and not just a bad dream.

Chapter 9

Realising the trench would possibly be shut down for several weeks and unsure whether they would be allowed to continue with the excavation of the rest of the site, Meera had informed the students that unfortunately, they would possibly no longer be able to finish the project. There was much disappointment in evidence, but as she pointed out,

'That's archaeology for you; you never know what's going to turn up.'

However, she assured them, she would certainly be asking the coroner to allow them to continue so they shouldn't have to wait long to find out whether they could carry on or not.

After speaking to the students, Meera rang the police to find out when the coroner was expected to arrive. As Alex wasn't there, she was put through to Sergeant Nugent, who told her that the deputy coroner had her number and would be contacting her directly to let her know when he intended to visit, which may not be until the following day. Meera explained she intended to keep everyone on site until she had spoken with the coroner, who, she hoped would allow them to finish the rest of the project.

'I think that may be difficult if the coroner decides that the burial needs further investigation. We will of course be calling in the osteo-archaeologist to oversee the excavation of the remains themselves,' Sally explained

'Very well, we'll have to wait and see what the deputy coroner has to say when he arrives and we'll take it from there,' Meera acknowledged and then hung up.

Turning to the others, Meera said,

'The deputy coroner will probably be here tomorrow so we can't do anything else today. Let's get packed up.'

Josh and Celine started organising the students to pack up the gear, but Pete hung back, obviously wanting to speak privately to Meera.

'Can I have a word, Meera,' Pete asked quietly.

Meera gestured for Pete to follow her out of the tent.

'Something bothering you?' she asked him.

After a short hesitation he replied,

'It just seems so weird. This place has given me the creeps from the start, but it's getting more intense with every hour that passes.'

'You've felt it too then?' Meera responded.

'You mean, you have as well?'

'I have. There's something very strange about this site Pete.'

'Definitely! I mean look what happened to that tarpaulin. I had secured it properly you know!'

'I do know because I saw you do it Pete. And that earring, appearing like that; it was definitely not there before we came back to the tent, was it?'

'Well I never saw it, but then I did leave sharpish, if you remember.'

'I do. What was all that about?' Meera queried.

'I don't know! I just suddenly felt ice cold and a feeling of intense sadness swept over me. I just had to get away.'

'Well, I've had similar sensations and that particularly terrifying dream about that damned blanket and the skeleton trying to force its way out of it, would you believe? I didn't think anyone else had felt it though.'

'Well, I certainly have, but good grief that nightmare sounds horrendous!'

Having stashed the last of the equipment into the bags and boxes, Josh came out to find them.

'That's it, we're ready when you are.'

'OK Josh,' Meera replied, then went over to let Sergeant Shapiro know that they would be leaving shortly.

He said they too would be leaving, after checking everything was secure, but a couple of his officers would be returning the next day.

The students were happy to sort out their own supper, and Meera and her team went on to the Crooked Gate. It was six thirty by the time they'd cleaned up and gone down to the bar where the landlady served them with their supper. After they'd all eaten, they settled down with drinks and the conversation turned inevitably to the mysterious grave.

'I just can't understand why anyone would want to dispose of a body by burying it in an archaeological site, risking that it might one day be re-excavated,' Josh declared.

'I know what you mean Josh, it's all very odd. Unless they needed to get rid of it quickly,' Celine suggested.

'What, by digging a hole several feet deep, throwing the body in wrapped in a blanket, and then filling it up again. Hardly a quick job!' Josh countered.

'But what if the hole was already there?' Pete asked.

'You mean, if it had already been excavated?'

'Yes, Celine, perhaps it had, already been excavated I mean.'

Realising the implication of what had just been said, all eyes now turned to Meera, whose stomach churned as she realised that the only excavation that had taken place to her knowledge at this site, was the one her father had carried out, and she knew what they must all be thinking.

Desperate to offer another explanation, she suggested it was possible that it had actually been a premeditated deposition of the remains, and that whoever had carried it out may have known that the site had already been excavated but hadn't realised that it might be reinvestigated at some later date. Maybe they thought that as it had once been done, it wouldn't need to ever be dug again.'

'But anyone who knows anything about archaeological training, would know that it was very likely that it would be re-dug by other students in the future,' Josh insisted.

'That's true,' Pete agreed.

'Well, maybe they didn't know that sometimes happened. Perhaps they knew nothing about archaeology,' Meera argued.

'Then how would they know that there had already been an archaeological investigation?' Celine asked.

'Well, if the burial is around thirty years old, if they lived around here, they may well have seen it taking place. When was your father's project Meera?'

'Thirty-five years ago. So that is possible Pete.'

However, glancing around she could see that none of them had found this explanation convincing.

Meera was relieved the old men weren't around that evening. She wasn't in the mood to be teased by them. In fact, this whole business was getting a bit too close to home. She felt confused and rather fearful. Logic was leading in a very unwelcome direction and one in which she did not wish to go.

She stood up and announced that she was off to bed and wished them all goodnight without further discussion. As she left, they glanced at one another, all suspecting that Meera had left to avoid further conversation about her father, which gave them all plenty of food for thought, although no one said any more about it that night.

It was with some trepidation that Meera placed her head on the pillow. She was terrified of having another nightmare. It had appeared so real the night before, and the conversation turning to her father and the possible re-use of a trench dug by his team, filled her with foreboding.

After an hour or so thinking about her father, she eventually drifted off. This time there was no nightmare, just a rather comforting dream featuring her father. She was a little girl, and they were in his office at the University. She was sitting by his side feeling very grown up as he showed her pictures in a book, explaining how the human body was constructed. She was happy to be there with him, feeling safe and loved as she always did. Then, suddenly, the skeleton on the page began to move, stretching out its hands towards her. Terrified once again, she screamed at it to go away and leave her alone. Then she was awake once more and trembling with fear.

'What the hell?!!' she said out loud, 'What's happening to me?!!'

Trying to clear her mind of what had just happened, she got up and took a walk to the bathroom where she swilled her face with cold water before returning quietly to her room. Another hour passed. She was trying desperately to think of anything other than the dig, her father, and the body in the grave, but the questions just kept coming. Loudest of all in her mind was the question of why her father had obviously not found the burial during his team's excavation of that particular trench. The trench was mentioned in his report but not the body. She knew the explanation she'd suggested to the others just didn't stack up, and she also knew that they knew it too. Finally, she managed to fall asleep with that question still revolving round her brain. Thankfully, there was no recurrence of the nightmare, but still her sleep was restless and shallow.

Chapter 10

As they were eating breakfast the next morning, Meera received a text from someone called Mr Grainger, which said that he was the Deputy Coroner. He told her that DI Scott had passed on her number and that he was letting her know that he would be on site by nine o'clock, if that was convenient. Meera texted back to confirm that she would indeed be on site by then.

In the event it was nine fifteen by the time Mr Grainger pulled into the carpark. Apparently, his satnav had directed him down a dead-end country lane, and he was not best pleased about it. He stepped into the tent with a distinctly irritated look on his face, and apologised to Meera who had stepped forward, offering her hand,

'Sorry I'm late Dr... Carter, is it? I'm afraid the technology let me down this time! '

'No problem,' Meera replied, 'these lanes are not easy to navigate, they all look the same and the hedges are so high that you can't even look out for landmarks. Would you like to take a look at the site, and then I can answer any questions you may have?'

'That would be very helpful Dr Carter.'

With that, she led him out to stand by the grave.

'This is the one. As you can see Mr Grainger, we had to carefully remove some of the remains of the blanket to discover if anything had been wrapped inside it. We unearthed the chest and skull, but as the body had not been buried in the usual east to west alignment, it was becoming obvious that this wasn't a Christian burial. We realised we could well be dealing with a crime scene, stopped work, and called the police. '

'I see, well, I'll need to take a closer look.'

He put on his protective suit and overshoes and pulling on his gloves, climbed down into the trench. After five minutes or so, he seemed satisfied that this burial would indeed need further investigation by the police.

'I am not a forensic archaeologist, but the circumstances of the burial and the presence of the car blanket definitely indicates that there may well have been some foul play here.'

Back in the tent, after removing his protective clothing, he explained the next procedure to Meera,

'As I'm sure you are aware Dr Carter, the trench, and ideally the whole site, must be preserved exactly as it is for the moment. I will report back to the coroner who will contact DI Scott to inform her of our decision, and she will get in touch with the osteo-archaeologist who will visit the site and decide how best to proceed to exhume the body for expert analysis and investigation of the crime, if indeed there proves to have been one.'

'Thank you, Mr Grainger. I am wondering whether it would be possible for us to proceed with the rest of the project on site. We have a group of students here who need to gain further experience before studying for their final year.'

'Can you show me exactly where they would be excavating?'

Meera took out the map with the trenches marked on it, pointing out that they would be several feet away from the burial. After going outside once more to see for himself exactly where they would be working, he announced that due to the proximity of the suspect burial to the rest of the excavations, he would rather leave that decision to the police and the osteo-archaeologist.

'I understand Mr Grainger. Of course, as you probably realise, this is a very important project for these third-year students.'

'Well, I'm sorry, but you'll have to leave everything exactly as it is. No one is allowed within the tapes for the moment. As I say, I will report back to the coroner, who I'm sure will be in touch with the police without delay, so you can expect a visit from the osteo-archaeologist, who will come up with a plan as to how the body will be examined forensically in situ before being removed for more comprehensive analysis. Well, I must be on my way Dr Carter,' he went on, 'and I hope my satnav will be more helpful on my return journey!'.

'I sincerely hope so,' Meera answered with a smile as they shook hands.

After he left, Meera gathered the students and her team together to explain that Mr Grainger had refused to allow them to continue with the project for the moment, insisting on the complete isolation of the site until the osteo-archaeologist had inspected the remains.

'In which case,' she told them, 'Perhaps you could use the rest of the day to carry out some online research, about the history of the church, the village and its surroundings. That will add context to your final reports about the project.'

Around mid-afternoon, Josh, Celine, and Pete took a group each and set about packing finds and equipment. Meera wasn't happy about the possibility of having to abandon the project, and went out onto the site, standing once more outside the tapes, looking down at the grave site. There were so many questions flying round her brain as she stood there. Who was this poor person who had apparently been thrown into a hole in the ground wrapped in a blanket? Was it a woman or a man? The earring may indicate the former, but best to keep an open mind. How had he or she died? Why did they have to die? Who wanted rid of them so badly that they had to be killed?

And of course, there was that one question that just wouldn't go away – how could her father have missed this? She still tried to convince herself that perhaps the body was buried after her father's project had been completed, but somehow that didn't stop the thought from springing back whenever she had a quiet minute to think. As she stood looking down at the remains, just visible in the surrounding earth, an overpowering feeling of fear gripped her. Was it a reflection of the fear the victim had felt as life had been forced from their body or was it fear of what she herself might discover as the story unfolded?

Just then she was dragged back to the moment by her phone insisting that someone was trying to call her. It was Sally Nugent.

'Good afternoon, Dr Carter,' she began, 'I've just spoken to the coroner's office, and they have confirmed that they believe the burial needs investigating as it does seem suspicious in many respects.'

'When do you think the osteo-archaeologist will arrive?'

'As it's quite late now, probably tomorrow. I'll send our forensics team to erect the tent around the burial right away. They should be with you within the hour. Anyway, you have our number if you need to get in touch.'

'Yes, I have,' Meera replied.

It was just an hour later that the team turned up to erect the tent, and she received a message later that afternoon to say that the osteo-archaeologist, Dr Felicity Butcher would indeed be visiting the following morning.

Chapter 11

After another restless night of strange images drifting in and out of her dreams, Meera woke early, even before her alarm went off. Eager to find answers to the questions still occupying her mind, she was downstairs and eating breakfast before anyone else appeared. She knew that once Dr Butcher had visited the site and agreed a plan to investigate the burial, hopefully she would begin to get some answers. However, as she sat drinking her tea, she was considering a dilemma that had arisen in her mind.

She had been hoping the police would allow her to work on the exhumation alongside their forensic archaeologists, but it had now occurred to her that if they were aware her father had worked on the original excavation, they may decide she shouldn't be allowed anywhere near this one. So, should she declare her possible conflict of interest up front? Almost before the question formed in her mind, she knew the answer. Professionally, she knew she must declare it. She was desperate though, to keep abreast of any findings that may come up in the course of the excavation.

At that moment, Pete appeared, declaring,

'You're early Meera! Still having trouble sleeping? This mysterious burial is unsettling, and as I've told you, this whole project has been giving me the creeps from the start. Anyway, maybe we'll begin to get some clues once forensics get their hands on it.'

As Pete was speaking, Meera had an idea,

'Well, we could do with someone working alongside them, and given my father's connection to the site, I'm pretty sure they'd rule me out. How would you feel about doing it?'

'I'd jump at the chance Meera. I'd relish the idea of working on it in the hope of finding out who it is, and maybe in the end helping to lay them to rest properly. I think it's the least we can do now that we've dug them up, as it were.'

'I agree. Right then, I'll put you forward to assist forensics with the excavation.'

'Thanks Meera, that's great. I could do with gaining some experience working with forensics in any case.'

'Well, the osteo-archaeologist is due to arrive this morning, so hopefully the forensic excavation should begin soon. In the meantime, we will probably be able to get on with investigating the rest of the site.'

In the event it was ten-thirty by the time Dr Felicity Butcher arrived. Meera recognised her immediately. She had been in the same cohort as herself at Bristol, although she hadn't been a particular friend of hers.

Meera introduced herself, but didn't mention their mutual experience of studying at Bristol, and Dr

Butcher didn't either. She probably doesn't recognise me, she thought.

Dr Butcher spent a good hour inspecting the site and the grave cut, paying particular attention to the position and context of the bones. When she'd finished, she returned to the tent and proceeded to complete several online forms on her laptop, sending copies to Meera and to the police.

'Well, I can confirm that in my opinion the body is likely to have been buried within the last forty years, and the contextual evidence indicates that we may possibly be dealing with a suspicious burial. I'll liaise with yourself and DI Scott to agree the best way to proceed, but I would suggest the next step should involve examination by the forensic archaeologists who will take samples from the skeleton and its surroundings to accurately determine the date when life was extinct. Once that's done, the body can be carefully and respectfully lifted and sent to the laboratory for further investigation.'

'Yes, of course,' Meera replied, 'and in the meantime I was hoping that my team and the students might be able to continue to excavate the rest of the site.?'

'Yes, that's fine, as long as security around the grave site is maintained, as I'm sure you know, Dr Carter.'

'Of course,' Meera confirmed.

With that, Dr Butcher left the site.

With some relief, Meera informed her team and the students that they were now free to restart the project.

Now that one of the three trenches was out of bounds, Meera decided that a further trench should be opened. Gathering the students and her team together again, she explained that as the burial trench was no longer accessible, she had decided that a fourth trench would be opened and asked them to suggest where that might be.

Belinda, always ready to jump in, piped up,

'Could we place one inside the building itself? Maybe across what looks as though it could be a kitchen area?'

'Thanks, Belinda, yes that's a good suggestion. Josh, would you mind marking it out. Same size as the others, of course.'

'Sure thing Meera, will do.'

With that, he asked Belinda to assist him, and they went off to do the job.

Just then Neil Cotton called to say that the forensics team of archaeologists would be with them in a day or two to begin the task of excavating the body, gathering any contextual evidence as they did so.

'Thanks for letting me know,' she replied, 'We'll be here if they need any assistance with anything.'

'That's good of you Dr Carter. I'll let them know.'

The rest of the day passed without interruption, all three teams working well, happy to be busy again. A few finds emerged from the newly excavated site inside the building, mainly pieces of medieval pottery which looked rather uninteresting to the untrained eye but were useful as evidence of domestic activity during the fourteenth century.

For the next couple of days Meera strove to keep her mind on her students and their activities but was still finding it difficult not to let her mind wander to the body in the grave, particularly as she had to pass it frequently as she moved around the site. Therefore, it was with some relief that she greeted the forensics team who, accompanied by Dr Butcher, finally arrived to begin their work.

After spending some time discussing with Hilary Black, the forensic archaeologist, how she wanted the investigation to be carried out, Dr Butcher left the site, saying that she'd be in touch and would, in any case, be back to see how things were progressing in a day or two. Hilary's team brought in a folding table which they erected at one end of the tent inside the church, presumably to receive any excavated bones or artifacts found in the vicinity of the remains.

Meera tentatively offered the services of Pete to assist with the excavation, stressing that he was an experienced archaeologist, who had agreed to help them if they wished.

'Thanks Meera. We can always use an extra pair of hands, particularly if they know what they're doing,' Hilary quipped, smiling.

Meera went to find Pete. He was supervising his students as they were excavating the foundation of a wall, presumably an inside wall of the building.

'Pete,' she called over to him, 'I've spoken to the forensics team, and they would be grateful if you could give them a hand.'

'Sure thing, Meera. My team appear to know what they're doing but perhaps you could just keep an eye on them?'

'Of course, Pete. Can you come and get kitted out now, forensics are just about to start.'

With that, Pete followed her back to the tent where she introduced him to Hilary.

'Glad to have you aboard Pete.'

The forensics team consisted of Hilary Black, a couple of assistants, and a photographer. Along with Pete, they lost no time getting kitted out in their Tyvek suits, gloves, and overshoes before stepping inside the forensics tent. Meera's team continued working on the other trenches, while the forensics team stepped down to take their first look at the skeleton.

Meera had asked Hilary if she would mind if she observed for a while as she was interested in studying their methods. Now wearing protective clothing, she stepped inside the tent. As she watched, they carefully removed the tarpaulin from the trench, and the forensic photographer took several photographs of the trench, as he continued to do throughout the excavation.

After carefully recording the contents of the grave, with Hilary closely observing, Mike, one of her assistants, further exposed the trunk area until it was fully visible. They paused while Angie, another of Hilary's team, drew a further diagram and another photograph was taken. Then Hilary asked Pete if he'd mind exposing the skull further.

Meera assumed that, as usually happened, once it had been fully recorded in situ, the skull would be removed and examined for indications of the age and sex of the individual, and any obvious signs of injury. Finally, Pete declared it was ready to be lifted. After it had been photographed and recorded in situ once more, assisted by Mike, Pete carefully lifted it and placed it face-up in a box containing protective padding. Meera looked at it intently and as she did so, momentarily, the image of a face flashed across it. She was shaken to the core and the colour drained from her face. It was only there for a split second, but the face bore an unmistakeable resemblance to her own!

'You alright Meera?' Hilary asked, 'You look as if you've seen a ghost!'

Meera, who was staring intently at the skull, shook her head, and in a trembling voice that belied her words, muttered,

'Errr! Yes, I'm fine, just a bit shocked – it looks like a young person, a young woman actually.'

As she spoke, she glanced at Pete who was also gazing at the face of the skull. Although he said nothing,

Meera could see that he too had unexpectedly felt or seen something.

Chapter 12

Hilary asked Pete to take the box and place it on the forensics finds table. As he passed Meera he looked into her eyes and could see fear, a fear he also felt once more as he glanced down at the skull.

Wanting to find out whether Pete had felt anything and desperate to talk to someone who might understand about what she'd just seen, Meera followed him into the tent. Thankfully, apart from Pete, it was empty. She had no desire to let anyone else know what had happened. They would think she was going out of her mind, and at this moment it certainly felt like she was. That face had been so real, and so familiar!

After placing the box on the table, Pete turned, and their eyes met. Without a word passing between them there was a mutual feeling of understanding and tears of gratitude welled up in Meera's eyes.

'What's happening to me Pete?' she asked quietly, 'I swear I saw a face when I looked at the skull, and it looked just like me!'

'I could see you were in a state of shock.'

'Did you see it too?'

'No, but I certainly felt something. Once again, I was filled with an overwhelming sadness and also, fear. I've never felt anything like it before when unearthing burials, but somehow this one is very different.'

'You can say that again! I just don't understand it. Do you think it might have something to do with the mystery of why my father didn't report it? Is my worrying about that playing tricks on my mind?'

'Well, that wouldn't explain why I'm getting these feelings too, would it?'

'That's true,' Meera agreed, then went on, 'At least if you're feeling it too, perhaps it means I'm not going mad!'

Pete smiled reassuringly.

'Of course you're not Meera! I guess we're both being a bit oversensitive for some reason.'

'I guess so,' Meera agreed, 'Come on, we'd better get back, Hilary will be wondering where you've got to.'

With that they left the tent and Pete climbed down into the trench to carry on excavating, this time working on the pelvic area.

Meera first went off to check on Pete's team to make sure they didn't need any instruction or advice. Then she decided that for the sake of her sanity, perhaps it would be wise to keep away from the burial for a while and concentrate on catching up with paperwork. Having been distracted by the grave site, she had rather neglected writing up her project notes, which she usually did every evening. Now she made a huge effort to forget the skull and the effect it had had on her and turning her back on the forensics finds table and its contents, removing her protective clothing she sat down, opened up her laptop and got to work.

She'd been working for a couple of hours on her computer when, checking the time, she was amazed to see that it was already three o'clock. and after saving her work, closed it down and went out on site to check on progress in the trenches. She was pleased with what they'd done and told them to start wrapping up.

As she walked back to the church, Hilary emerged from inside the forensics tent explaining,

'We've almost finished here for the moment Meera.'

'Oh, that's quick,' Meera replied, 'do you intend to leave the rest of the skeleton in situ?'

'Oh no, it's just that we need to carry out some tests on the skull and one of the long bones back in the lab, and then we'll be back to remove the rest of it and the remains of the blanket of course.'

'This is looking more and more like a crime scene, isn't it?' Meera suggested.

'Well, until we've done a complete examination, I can't say one way or another but given the way it was buried and the lack of a coffin, it certainly looks suspicious.'

'How long has it been in the ground, do you think?'

'Again, until we do some analysis, I can't say Meera, but as the osteo-archaeologist suggested, the condition of the bones indicates several years at least, maybe even three or four decades.'

'I guess you'll be able to pin it down pretty accurately when you analyse it more thoroughly?'

'Well, we will get the skull back to the lab today along with one of the long bones, and we may get an indication of the cause of death, although this may be difficult until we examine the whole skeleton. However, as I'm sure you're aware, if we can extract DNA from the bone marrow it may give us an identity, and from the teeth, the isotopes in the enamel could provide an indication of the geographical origin of the deceased.'

'Of course, and how long will it take before your results are in?'

'Could be a couple of days for the DNA, longer for accurate isotopic dating, maybe a couple of weeks, but I'll keep you updated. When is your dig due to be completed?'

'Four or five weeks I should think,' Meera replied.

'Well, I'm pretty sure we'll have the results by then,' Hilary assured her.

After securing the screen around the grave, Hilary and her team left. They all, apart from Pete, of course, were from the local area and weren't staying at the pub. They took the box containing the skull, and a bone from the forearm for analysis, and left, leaving Meera relieved that there was no chance of her setting eyes on the skull again, for now at least. However, she was also left with a deep feeling of loss, of something missing. Worse than that, she now had a throbbing sensation in her left forearm. Earlier, she had noticed it was the radius bone from the left arm that Hilary had taken for analysis. Now she was utterly spooked.

She was desperate to speak to Pete again. It seemed he was the one person who might empathise with what she was feeling. It would be difficult though, without involving Josh and Celine, and she certainly didn't want to do that. She just hoped an opportunity would arise later that evening.

As it happened, they had just finished supper when Meera's phone rang. It was Belinda. Martin, one of the students, had accidentally almost cut the top of one of his fingers off as he was washing up the pots from supper. Belinda said it looked pretty bad, and was half severed. Unfortunate for Martin, but Meera immediately spotted her opportunity and asked Pete if he would drive her to the barn and probably to the A&E department to get Martin's wound dealt with. He could park up, she added, while she went into the emergency department with the young man. He readily agreed, although Josh also volunteered, and there was a moment of awkwardness as Meera declined his offer in favour of Pete taking her.

Once they were in the car, Meera told him about the feelings of loss she experienced once the skull had been removed and the throbbing in her arm, which was still continuing.

'Of course, you know which bone they took along with the skull, don't you?'

'I do,' Pete replied, 'because I excavated it myself, and I swear that skeleton wasn't too pleased about it. There was a distinct malevolent feeling as I lifted it away.'

'Oh my God, Pete!' Meera exclaimed, 'Look, I have to ask you this, because I'm sure there is something at work here that I've never encountered before; but do you believe in life after death?'

'Well, I never have, but now I'm not too sure!'

At that moment they pulled up outside the barn and went inside to see how things were with Martin. As soon as Meera saw his finger it was clear it would need stitching, so a visit to the hospital was definitely essential.

Chapter 13

It was after midnight by the time they dropped Martin back at the barn, having had his finger successfully stitched. After they had reinstalled him safely, ensuring that he had pain killers to get him through the night, they left to make their way back to the Crooked Gate. Arriving at the carpark, by mutual silent consent, they remained sitting quietly in the car, then both spoke at once,

'Sorry, you first,' Pete said quickly.

'Well, I was just going to say that I'm so grateful that you seem to be experiencing something of what I'm also going through.'

'And that goes for me too,' Pete replied.

They glanced across at each other and both realised for the first time that their connection wasn't just about what was happening at the dig. As the days had gone by, they had both felt drawn into something else. It was as though a thread between them was growing shorter and shorter, gradually bringing them closer. This realisation came as a shock to Meera, who wasn't sure whether any intimate relationship with Pete would be particularly ethical. She was in a senior position to him after all, and able to influence the progress of his career, for better or worse. Similar thoughts were going through Pete's mind also, and the last thing he wanted to do was to place Meera in a difficult position.

They both, simultaneously, decided they needed to step back from this situation, but in the end, it was Meera that broke the silence and said,

'Well, we'd better get inside,' and without further ceremony hastily opened the car door and got out.

Pete sat for a moment, thinking about what had just happened, before following Meera to the pub door. Before they'd left to pick Martin up, the landlady had given them the code for the lock. Meera now opened the door. Pete followed her in and as she reached the stairs she turned and smiled at him. His heart beat a little faster as he returned her smile.

'Goodnight then,' Meera whispered softly, 'thanks for taking me tonight, and thanks for being so supportive,'

'My pleasure Meera, that's what friends are for, after all,' he replied quietly.

Watching her climb the stairs, he tried to make sense of his emotions. Was it simply that he felt a natural protectiveness towards a colleague who was going through stress or was there more to it than that. He was undeniably attracted to Meera. He admired her intellect. He also admired the way she had been leading the project, ensuring everyone was heard and involved in decision making.

Of course, he'd admired colleagues before, but never had he felt like this. Perhaps, he thought, the strange effect the dig was having on them both had something to do with it. After all, shared experiences can create a kind of bond between people. Maybe that was it. The rather clandestine quality to their growing relationship was generating a certain excitement between them. As he now followed Meera up the stairs, he decided that was a plausible explanation, and determined to do nothing about it, but just to let things lie and see how they developed.

For her part, Meera's emotions were in turmoil as she prepared for bed. The incident with the skull and the sensation in her arm had disturbed her deeply, particularly the face of the young woman that had flashed before her as she glanced at the skull. Although she had immediately thought it was her own face, now she wasn't so sure. The dark complexion was certainly similar to hers but the features less so. What did it mean? And now, on top of that, what on earth had just happened?

She'd had relationships before, but had never been particularly emotionally involved, and had certainly never felt the way she had just felt in the car. Could it have been because her emotions were already heightened by this blasted dig? Trying desperately to apply her usually logical brain to the situation, she too decided it would be wise to try to calm down and see how things developed. However, she couldn't deny that she was looking forward to having Pete around for the next few weeks at least. Somehow, she felt that she may well need a confidante and a good friend before the truth behind this particular mystery was known.

Neither Pete nor Meera slept much that night. Meera couldn't dismiss the image of a young woman, terrified and alone with her killer, and pleading to be allowed to live, that kept springing up each time she started to drop off, bringing her back to consciousness once again. As for Pete, although he slept, his dreams were full of Meera and how she repeatedly begged him for help, although she never said why she needed him to rescue her, or from what.

When Pete came down to breakfast, Josh was already there.

'Well, well,' he said with a grin, 'what happened to you two last night?'

Much to his horror, Pete actually flushed, mumbling,

'Oh, er... it took ages at A& E, you know what it's like once you get into those places.'

Josh, still grinning, commented in a tone that conveyed a wealth of meaning,

'Yeah! Right!'

Then deciding to spare Pete further embarrassment, he went on,

'Anyway, did Martin get his finger reattached?'

'Well, it wasn't actually chopped off,' Pete replied, smiling now, thankful that Josh's attention had switched to Martin, 'although it needed quite a lot of stitches. I expect that's going to be the end of his digging on this project. He'll probably be confined to clerical duties for the duration.'

At that moment Celine and Meera appeared. With a quick 'Good morning' to Pete and Josh, they went straight to the service table to help themselves to breakfast, before sitting down together at the table under the window.

Meera felt that with all the goings on with the grave cut, she had rather neglected engaging with Celine. She knew a little about her. She had married her partner Diana about three years ago and they were hoping to adopt a baby.

'How's Diana?' Meera enquired, 'I don't expect she's too happy about you being away from home for the summer?'

'Well, I don't think she is, but it's what she signed up for when she married me, isn't it?' Celine replied, smiling. 'But that may change of course, once we get the baby?'

'Of course, I had heard. How's it going?' Meera queried.

'Well, apparently, they do have a child in mind and we're due to have a meeting with social services in a couple of weeks. In fact, I was going to let you know that I'll probably need to take two or three days off, later this month.'

'Of course, no problem. You must be getting very excited.'

'We are of course, but it's still pretty daunting, taking on responsibility for another person's life.'

'I imagine it must be.'

'Forgive me, and tell me to mind my own business,' Celine went on, 'but have you never fancied having a family?'

'Well, I guess I haven't really given it much thought. I've been too busy climbing the greasy pole to think about marriage and children. 'Course I realise that the body clock is ticking fast!'

'Yeah Meera, don't leave it too late,' Celine responded, 'Still, I'm sure some handsome archaeologist will sweep you off your feet before too long.'

Meera glanced across to where Josh and Pete were sitting and was embarrassed to find Pete, who had obviously been listening in to their conversation, gazing straight at her. Looking quickly away she rapidly changed the subject, saying,

'Well, I'm sure you and Diana will make great parents. I hope all goes well for you.'

However, she couldn't help noticing that Josh was smiling knowingly in Pete's direction.

God, she thought, is it that obvious?!

Chapter 14

The police had called Alex to ask her to go down to Tidmouth to formally identify her mum and dad. She had agreed to go the next day. Now she was full of foreboding as she lay beside Dave in bed that night. How would she cope with seeing them, pale, cold and lifeless. She struggled to stop her mind bringing up images of them lying in the morgue. In the course of her job, many times she had watched others struggling with seeing a loved one like that, but never had she truly realised the depth of their pain and feeling of helplessness in the face of it. Eventually she had managed a couple of hours sleep, but of course as soon as she opened her eyes the nightmare, for that is what it felt like, began all over again. Her mum and dad had gone. Forever. Once again, the finality of death struck her like a thunderbolt, but there was nothing she could do about it. The only option was acceptance, and she wasn't ready to do that yet.

'Are you sure you're ok to drive down to Tidmouth today love?' Dave ventured.

'I am Dave. I must. I have to formally identify them, and to find out precisely what happened and exactly how they died.'

Once again, Dave had to accept that when his wife made up her mind, it was impossible to get her to change it.

'OK, I do understand,' he responded. 'Don't worry about the kids. I can work from home today and, I'll keep them off school. Give them some time to process it all.'

'Yes, I agree, but if you think they're alright, I do think they should go back tomorrow, if only to give them something else to think about.'

'I'm sure you're right, but I'll see how they are today before deciding. How long do you think you'll be down there?'

'Only a couple of days. Once I've got the answers I need, I must check in with work. This new case is a tricky one.'

'Well, there are plenty of people to be getting on with it, so try not to worry about that. You've got enough to deal with right now.'

'I hear you. Don't worry, I'll be fine you know,' she assured him, as she stood up to prepare for her trip.

'I know you will,' he agreed, standing up and pulling her into a gentle embrace.

Alex had booked into an hotel in Tidmouth. She just could not face staying at her parent's house on her own. Sitting in the car now, she took one last look at the tidy semi-detached house where she had grown up, on the outskirts of the town. The house had represented everything that was good in her childhood. An only child, she had been as close to her parents as a child could ever be. They had created a world of fun and opportunity for her without over-indulgence. They had taught her self-reliance and self-belief that could only come from feeling loved and cherished.

Now her life would have to go on without them and it hurt. God, how it hurts, she thought. She had done and seen everything she needed to over the last few days. She had visited them in the mortuary, thankfully finding them both looking peaceful, with no sign of the traumas they must have endured. The injuries were internal, the pathologist had told her, their internal organs damaged badly by the impact of the crash. She had spoken to the police who assured her that they both died within seconds and would not have suffered. They assured her that they were carrying out a thorough investigation and would be reporting in due course to the coroner, but at the moment, it appeared that her father had pulled out into oncoming traffic at a crossroads.

Devastated and feeling it would be too painful to visit the crash site, she had made her way to their home in Cherry Tree Drive which was ordeal enough. Its emptiness crushed her and as soon as she'd stepped into the lounge, her emotions had taken over as she looked down at her dad's favourite chair and cried out,

'Dad, what have you done! You should have taken more care!' thumping the cushions angrily as the tears flowed.

She had needed to visit the house to retrieve the documents she would need to organise the funerals. It was so typical of her mum, she thought, to have made sure everything was safely tucked away. A couple of years ago she had shown them to her, saying,

'When you need them, you'll find everything together in this box.'

She remembered saying,

'Good grief mum, let's not talk about that, you'll be around for plenty of years yet!'

'Well,' Dorothy had replied wisely, 'None of us know about that, do we?'

Now Alex glanced down at the box on the seat beside her and once more tears ran down her cheeks.

It was around eleven when she arrived home. The house was empty, the children probably at school and Dave at work. She set the box carefully down on her dressing table in the bedroom. She couldn't face opening it right now.

She showered and changed then went down to the kitchen and made herself a sandwich and a cup of tea, intending to ring her team at the station when she'd finished. She wanted to keep in touch with developments and was ready now to get back to work, at least until the inquest and the funerals.

At that moment, Sally Nugent was sitting in the office, checking out the history of Old St Paul's when Neil walked in.

As soon as he stepped inside the office, Sally could tell that he was bringing important news.

'What?' she asked brusquely, 'Have you found something?'

'Not sure,' he replied, 'but I think you'll be interested to hear that the person who ran the last project on that site, thirty-five years ago, was none other than Professor Robert Carter.'

'What! Any relation?'

'Can't say at this stage.'

'More than a coincidence though, surely?!'

Sally felt that Alex would definitely want to be told about this immediately and said so to Neil.

'I'll give her a ring now Neil. and ask her what she wants us to do about it. Give me a few minutes, will you?'

After Neil had left the office, Sally rang Alex's number.

'Hi Sally, I was just about to call you. Has something come up?' Alex answered.

'Well, I'm sorry to bother you, but I was sure you'd like to know about this. The only other excavation that has been carried out on the Old St Paul's site, is a project run by Professor Robert Carter, thirty-five years ago.'

'What! Any relation?'

'Well, we don't know for certain yet but surely, that is pretty likely?'

'Of course! Well, if he is related to her, I wonder why the good doctor didn't' mention that little tidbit?'

'How do you want us to handle it Boss?'

'I think it's time we had a chat with Dr Carter,' she went on. I've got a couple of things to do here this morning, but I'll be in around one-ish and we'll get over to the site.'

'Are you sure you're ready to come in Boss? I could handle it myself, taking Neil with me, if you like.'

'No Sally, I'm fine. In fact, I think I need to keep busy and until the funerals there's not much I can do, I'll see you later.'

'Ok Boss. In the meantime, I'll get the team to take a look at Professor Robert Carter.'

'Good idea Sally, the more we know about him the better.'

As Alex drove to the station, glad of the diversion, she was trying to work out possible connections between the Professor, the body, and the Doctor, maybe even the daughter of the Professor! The coincidence was just too much. Firstly, she realised, they needed to know exactly when the person had died. Was it before or after the Professor had carried out the excavation? If it was before, had he discovered the body? If so, why had it not been reported to the coroner? And now, it was possibly his daughter who had actually discovered it. Had she had an idea it was there, somehow? Had he ever told her about it? So many questions!

Alex had called ahead to say she was on her way and Sally was waiting in front of the station building as she pulled up. As they were driving along, Sally took the first opportunity she'd had to express her sympathy face to face for the loss of Alex's parents. Then she went on to fill Alex in, about what they had managed to find out so far about Professor Carter. She explained that he was an archaeologist and had spent several years working for the Ministry of Defence, carrying out excavations of the war dead in various places around the world. On returning to the UK, he had taken up a post at Bristol University, and apparently the project at Old St Paul's had been his first after returning from India.

'And where is he now?' Alex asked.

'Unfortunately, he died four years ago, so no chance of questioning him about the body.' Sally explained.

Chapter 15

I t was two o'clock by the time they arrived at the site. They found Meera at her computer inside the tent.

'Inspector! Has something happened? Do we have an identity for the deceased?'

'Dr Carter. Good afternoon. This is DS Sally Nugent,' she went on, gesturing towards Sally, 'No, we don't have any further information about the identity of the body. We are still waiting for test results.

Meera nodded in Sally's direction then continued,

'Of course. Well, how can I help you?'

'Right now, we are looking into the history of the site. What do you know about any previous excavations here?'

Meera hesitated momentarily, realising that the time had come to tell them about her father's project. Desperately trying to sound calm and matter of fact, finally she said,

'Well, as I'm sure you know, or will soon find out, the only previous excavation of this site that we know of was my father's, Professor Robert Carter, which he carried out about thirty-five years ago.'

Feigning a shocked expression, Alex said,

'Well, that's quite a coincidence Dr Carter. How come?'

'I know it sounds rather pathetic, but my father died four years ago, and I'm not sure why, it just felt right, like perhaps he would somehow know that I've finally achieved my goal in this job, to gain my PhD and to run my own project.'

Thoughts of Ted and Dorothy tried to intrude into Alex's mind, but she managed to push them aside. This was no time to go down that road, she told herself firmly.

'I see,' she responded, 'and would there be a copy of his report somewhere?'

'Yes, of course, I have a copy on my laptop.'

'And does it mention anything about a body being located?'

Meera's stomach churned. She could see that Alex was losing no time in getting to the nub of the question. Trying to steady her voice which was suddenly quivering slightly, betraying her nervousness, she replied,

'Errr... Although it does refer to a trench being excavated it doesn't mention a burial.'

'Mmm... that's odd, don't you think Sally?' Alex said, turning to look at Sally, who nodded in agreement.

'I know, and of course, I've been wondering about that myself. I think the remains must have been deposited after my father's dig finished. What other explanation could there be?'

'Our job, Dr Carter,' Alex replied rather ominously, 'is to find that out. Would you mind forwarding a copy of the report? My email address is on my card,' she added, handing Meera her business card.

'Oh, err... Yes, of course,' Meera replied, annoyed with herself that there was still a rather nervous quality to her voice.

Alex and Sally were standing over Meera, which was making her even more nervous, although she couldn't think for the life of her why she should be. To normalise the situation, she stood up and asked whether they would like a drink.

In view of the possibly difficult conversation she was about to have with her, Alex accepted her offer and she and Sally sat down while Meera made them a coffee.

'So, as you can probably appreciate Dr Carter, we have something of a problem here.'

'Well, I can see that in the circumstances, at least until you can establish that what we've found was deposited after my father had finished his project, you probably won't want me anywhere near the grave.'

'I'm grateful you are so understanding Dr Carter.'

'In fact, in anticipation of your possible concerns, I haven't entered the trench personally since we called you in. Pete, one of my assistants, has been helping Hilary with the excavation.'

'To be honest, Dr Carter, I think no-one who is working with you should be assisting the forensics team. As you will appreciate, that may still cause a conflict-of-interest situation to arise. Is he on site now?'

'He is,' Meera replied. 'Perhaps you'd better speak to him yourself, Inspector.'

'Indeed,' she replied, then turning to Sally, instructed her to go and ask Pete to join them in the tent.

A couple of minutes later she returned, followed by Pete.

When he looked at Meera, he could tell she was stressed.

'What's the problem?' he asked of Alex.

'No problem Mr ...'

'Shore,' Pete interjected.

'Sorry, no problem, Mr Shore.'

'Then how can I help you Inspector?'

'Can I take it that, as Hilary Black isn't on site until tomorrow, you aren't working on the burial trench today?'

'That's right,' Pete replied, 'I'm supervising the students on the trench over the main building.'

'Well, thank you for helping forensics out but I have to ask you not to do so again.'

'Whyever not? If you don't mind me asking.'

'Your connection with Dr Carter could jeopardize the reliability of any evidence you might discover.'

'Why is that, exactly?'

'Because of the possible connection of Dr Carter's father with the person in the grave.'

'What!' Pete exclaimed, 'I fail to see why that would make any difference.'

'I'm sorry Mr Shore, but you must let me be the judge of that.'

Pete looked at Meera, wanting to take his lead from her. A slight shrug of her shoulders told him all he needed to know, and he said,

'Of course, Inspector. Is that all?'

'For the moment, thankyou Mr Shore.' Alex replied.

Pete left the tent and Alex turned to Meera once again.

'Regarding the body Dr Carter. Did your father ever mention to you about finding remains in the trench?'

'No, he didn't Inspector, and I can't believe they were even there when his team carried out the excavation. They can't have been or as I say, he would surely have reported it. In fact, he never spoke to me about the project on this site. It wasn't until I was doing research to determine where to locate this student dig, that I discovered that he had excavated here at all.'

'One other thing,' Alex continued, 'Do you know who else was working on the site with your father?'

'Well, the report does mention several people but the only one I recognised is Leonard Larkin. He is now Professor Len Larkin working in the anthropology department of Bristol University.'

'Thank you, that's helpful. Well, I think that's all for the moment Dr Carter. The test results on the samples of the remains should be with us soon, which should provide some answers. We'll be in touch when we have them, and we'll probably need to talk to you again. Will you still be working on site?'

'Well, we'll be here for another four or five weeks at least.'

As Alex and Sally stood up to leave, Alex said,

'Very well, we'll be in touch.'

On the way back to the station, Sally asked,

'What did you make of all that Boss? I thought she seemed very nervous when she told us about her father.'

'She did Sally, but perhaps that's not surprising. Knowing, as she obviously did, that her father had dug the site before, but not reported finding any remains, she must be asking herself the same questions we are asking. How could he not have found it and if he had, why hadn't he reported it?'

'My thoughts exactly, which mean he could be connected in some way to the death of the individual. Clearly an unthinkable scenario for any daughter.'

Chapter 16

Back in the office, Alex called a meeting of all the team. Besides Sally Nugent, Neil Cotton, and Mark Jones, they had been joined by Ida Bromsgrove, a trainee detective who had just completed her Detective Training course and was now on probation. She seemed keen to impress, bright and helpful.

Before Alex began, she thanked everyone for their sympathy, then went straight into recapping what they knew so far, about the body at Old St Paul's, which wasn't very much.

'As you all know the human remains were found during excavations next to the ruins of Old St Paul's church, Little Stretford. You may think that being next to a church, this wouldn't be surprising. However, it was found outside the burial ground, wrapped in a blanket, and buried under three feet of soil. The body was not aligned east to west, as is usual for a Christian burial, and furthermore, being wrapped in a car blanket indicates that it was buried relatively recently. Forensics are testing samples as we speak and we expect to have DNA results soon as well as a definitive age for the person at death, cause, and date of death, and possibly ethnicity and areas of the world where they had lived.

'Other information which may be relevant has also come to light. Dr Meera Carter is the project manager of the current excavation, but her father, Professor Robert Carter carried out the only previous excavation on the site, and that was thirty-five years ago.'

'That's quite a coincidence isn't it Boss,' Neil said, 'Did Dr Carter know about that?'

'She did, and she's sending his report through to us, but apparently there is no mention of a body in it, which is very odd indeed. It may be that he didn't excavate in that area of the site at all, or alternatively the remains may have been deposited after he'd finished his project there. Either way, we need to find out as much as we can about Professor Carter and, for that matter, Dr Carter too. Mark, did you get anything from misspers?

'No, nothing has turned up so far Boss.'

'Maybe we ought to widen the search. The victim may have come from anywhere. But wait until we have more details so that we can target the research before you do that.'

'OK Boss,' Mark replied.

'In the meantime, perhaps you and Ida could look into the Carters. Pull up anything and everything you can find on those two.'

'Will do Boss.'

'OK everyone, I'll speak to you again once the results are in.'

After DI Scott and her sergeant had left the site, Meera had pulled up the file of her father's project report and was about to email it over to the police when something stopped her. She was desperate to find an explanation as to why her father hadn't mentioned the burial. What if, she thought, the trench he'd opened wasn't the one containing the body after all? Maybe it was a different one. She set about re-reading the file in detail. Since finding the body she had only skipped over it, specifically looking for information about a burial, and nothing had jumped out at her. Now, studying it more carefully, she did find a reference to a trench which had contained not a burial, but evidence of Iron Age activity. So, he had found archaeology in a trench after all, but not, perhaps, in this one. If that was true, there should be evidence in the technical data of a second area showing disturbance within the cloisters.

She took out the geophysics printout which had been produced for her project and studied it carefully, then went out and called Pete over to the tent. She asked him if he could see any other areas that might indicate an earlier trench having been excavated, explaining that she was wondering whether her father had investigated a different area. After studying it carefully, while admitting he wasn't an expert, he said he could see an area quite near to one of the cloister walls that could possibly be worth looking at.

'Maybe that's it!' Meera said with mounting excitement. 'The trench he refers to in his report must be that one, and not the one we've excavated at all! Don't you see Pete, that means it's got nothing to do with my father.'

'That's what it would indicate, but doesn't the report say exactly where his trench is located?'

'Well, unfortunately, the diagram of the site wasn't with the rest of the report, so we only have his description of the trench and not its exact position.'

'That's a bit odd in itself though, don't you think, Meera?'

'Mmm, but it would have been on a separate sheet from the report itself and must have become separated from it. I ought to go back to the archives and try to find it.'

'Alternatively, we could excavate the possible disturbance near the cloister wall to see if it is due to archaeology in a previous excavation, or just a natural phenomenon.'

'True, and that would probably be quicker. After all, the diagram may not even be there after all this time.'

'OK, shall I start on that tomorrow? It's getting a bit late now. I could pull a couple of my team off my trench for a few hours in the morning if you like.'

'Let me sleep on it Pete. Meanwhile, I need to get this file sent over to the police. Thanks for your input though, I'm finding it difficult to be objective regarding this damned burial.'

'Ok Meera, shall I tell everyone that you want them to start packing up?'

'Yes please Pete, I've certainly had enough of all this for today!'

With that, still with some apprehension, Meera attached her father's report to an email addressed to DI Scott, then hurriedly clicked 'send' before she changed her mind.

That night the nightmares returned with a vengeance. This time, it seemed more real than ever. Her father was there, with a figure who was standing with its back to her and as it had long dark hair, she assumed it must be her mother. They were standing in the ruins of the church. It was dark, but with a full moon. They seemed to be arguing, shouting at one another although Meera could hear no sound. To her horror, her father pushed the figure, and it stumbled backwards, towards her. As it fell on its back she saw its upturned face, but it wasn't a face at all, it was the skull of a skeleton. It held out its arms to Meera pleading for help, then suddenly it had hold of Meera's ankle, trying to pull her down towards it. She struggled to pull free of its grip, but it held her firm. She was slowly being pulled further down into what had now become a deep, black hole in the ground. She screamed, and was suddenly awake, terrified, and sweating with fear.

'What the hell was all that about,' she mumbled as she heard a soft knocking on her door.

'Meera, are you alright?'

It was Pete, who had just been passing on his way to bed.

'I'm ok Pete, just another damned nightmare.'

'Can I get you anything? A drink or something?'

'No thanks, I'm fine. Really.'

With that, he said goodnight and carried on to his room.

I can't help thinking that damned skeleton is trying to tell me something, she thought to herself. The fact that her father had figured prominently once again she put down to having been discussing him with DI Scott and then of course, studying his project report. In any event, she thought, I'll be glad when we get some answers and can eventually lay the thing to rest. Maybe then it won't be bothering me again.

Chapter 17

As Meera and the others were eating breakfast, Hilary, eager to make a start on studying the skull and forearm bone, was already in the lab. She decided the most important information the police would need would be the DNA results and a probable date and possible cause for the death of the deceased.

She instructed her colleague Chris to clean the long bone carefully and drill out some of the bone tissue to prepare for DNA analysis which was to be carried out by a consultant geneticist she had used several times before.

'I wonder if you'd mind popping it over to Mr Ford in person when it's ready Chris. I know the police are keen not to have any delay on this.'

Right on cue, there was a knock on the window of the lab door and Neil Cotton strode in.

'Hello Mrs Black. Do you have any results for us yet?' he asked briskly.

'Well, we've got the skull and I'm just about to make a start assessing it. Chris has been preparing a bone sample for DNA analysis.'

'Great, but what can you tell me at this moment.'

'Well, in my opinion it does look like a female, but we'll know for certain when the DNA results come back. In the meantime, once we've excavated the pelvic area fully, that will also give us a stronger indication of the sex of the individual.'

'And what about a date for the death and subsequent burial?'

'Again, I'll need to do more detailed analysis, but from the general condition and context of the remains I'm guessing, the 80's or 90's, so I would estimate somewhere between thirty and forty years.'

'Cause of death?'

'Not yet but I haven't had a chance to study the skull thoroughly. That's my next job.'

'Okay. Any clues about ethnicity?'

'Give me a break young man! I may be good, but I ain't that good,' Hilary quipped.

'Oh of course, point taken. I guess the DNA results will be an important key. How long do you think it will take?'

'A couple of days if we're lucky, or up to a week if they're very busy.'

'Well please can you stress the urgency Mrs Black? We need to find out who this woman is as soon as possible. She may have family who've been searching for her for decades!'

'I certainly will, of course.'

'Right, well, I'll leave you to it then,' Neil said decisively then disappeared as quickly as he'd arrived.

Hilary glanced over to Chris, saying,

'You heard all that? They're impatient already! These coppers have no idea, have they?'

'They certainly haven't! Anyway, I should have the samples ready by mid-morning tomorrow.'

'OK, well I'll be taking my team back on site tomorrow to carry on with the excavation of the rest of her, so if you could make sure the results get across to the genetics people, hopefully they can start work on it. I'll drop them an email to put them in the picture as to the urgency.'

'OK Hilary, no problem,' Chris replied.

Hilary spent the rest of the day dealing with the skull. After cleaning it carefully she began to scrutinise it more carefully. She had already noted the shape of the brow ridge, which was fairly flat. The bones around the chin area further indicated that it was indeed a female.

All the teeth were present and in good order with little wear, possibly indicating a largely vegetarian diet. Nowadays many people are vegetarians she thought, but thirty years ago it wasn't so common. Could this indicate a possible connection with an Asian religion? Well, she considered, isotopic analysis should indicate whether she had spent any length of time in an Asian country and maybe even which one. The fact that all the teeth including the wisdom teeth were present, suggested that this person was most likely over twenty-five years old. Eventual examination of the rest of the skeleton would probably enable her to be more precise as to the age at death.

Examining the surface of the skull carefully, Hilary could find no sign of trauma. There would appear to have been no violent attack on the skull at least, so the cause of death was yet to be determined.

As it was so well preserved, she knew it would be possible to have facial reconstruction carried out by the maxillofacial unit, but that would be expensive and not something she could authorise. That would be down to the police if they decided they needed to go down that route. She suspected they would be hoping the DNA results would be conclusive enough in themselves.

Alex had arrived in the office early and now called a meeting of the team to discuss the next steps regarding the identification of the body. and they all gathered in the outer office to await her thoughts on the approaches she had decided to take.

She began by instructing them, to their amusement, to do some digging about the site. Was this a site that had been excavated by anyone else apart from Professor Robert Carter and his daughter Dr Meera Carter, she queried. She said that apparently the University used several sites in the area to offer training opportunities for their budding archaeologists.

'We know this is one of them,' she went on. 'If anyone else was ever involved in working on a project there, is it possible to find and speak to them?'

She also asked them to find out what they could about Dr Meera Carter. She seemed pretty competent and switched on she told them, but once or twice she had seemed rather nervous. Surely, she must be used to digging up old bones. So why the nervousness?

'The genetics people are working on analysing the DNA results right now and we should have the results within a day or two, but meanwhile, there's plenty we can be doing, and we'll meet again tomorrow morning at nine for an update so let's get on with it.'

With that, Alex left the meeting, and the detectives set to work.

Chapter 18

Alex opened her eyes and threw her arm across Dave who was still gently snoring beside her. Then, of course, it hit her once again. Her mum and dad were gone! It was over a week since Dave had come to the station to tell her, and she fought back the tears once more, and forced herself to bring her thoughts back to the case. Sally had called her last evening to let her know that the DNA results on the body had been sent to the geneticist who expected to let them have information on them the next day. She had told Sally that she'd be in first thing next morning.

Kissing Dave lightly on his shoulder she carefully slid out of bed and padded across to the bathroom. As she came out, Dave was climbing out of bed.

'Are you sure you need to go in love, can't you take some time off?' he asked.

'You know I can't do that right now. I must move this case on. The results from the lab are in and I need to check them out. Hopefully, I won't need to be in all day, and I'll try to get back by the time the kids are home. If you don't get a chance to find out when we can go ahead with the funerals, I'll do it then.'

'Well, I'll try, and I'll text you if I get any information.'

'Ok love, thanks.'

With that, Alex dressed quickly and went to call the children. As soon as she'd set out their breakfast and grabbed a slice of toast, she called up to Dave to say she was off.

'OK love, see you later,' she heard him call back as she picked up the car keys off the hall table and stepped out of the house, closing the door behind her.

When she arrived at the station, Sally was already there and speaking on the phone.

'OK, thanks, see you later then,' Sally said, just as Alex came through the door.

'Morning Sally, was that the geneticist?'

'It was Boss, and it sounds like they have found a couple of possible matches. He'll be over at around ten this morning.'

'Excellent! Maybe we can start to get somewhere with it at last. What about any other results from the lab? Do we know the sex and maybe a date for the burial of the body yet?'

'I'll give Hilary a ring, shall I?'

'Yes, please do Sally.'

Five minutes later Sally was back.

'Hillary is certain it's female, but nothing yet on date of death. That's going to take a bit longer.'

'Have we found anything more out about the Carters?'

'Not much to find apparently. Neither of them is on our system. We know he travelled around the world quite a bit before settling back down in the UK, and was quite eminent in the archaeology field, writing a few books and papers.'

'OK, well let's keep digging for the moment,' Alex suggested, then got on with some of the paperwork that was beginning to pile up on her desk, given her absences of the past week.

At around ten-fifteen, Mr Ford, the geneticist arrived. As Neil ushered him in to Alex's office, he introduced himself.

'Well, thank you for coming in Mr Ford.'

'No problem, I had to come over on another matter, so I thought I'd drop my report in at the same time.'

'And what have you found?'

'I found two partial matches. They seem to be siblings, one male and one female.'

'Any idea of where we might locate them?'

'Well, my analysis indicates that the woman was originally from South Asia, most probably east India.'

'That's interesting, and is it possible to say whether she was a recent immigrant to this country?'

'That will need further tests.'

'And do we have actual identities for the siblings yet?'

'Hopefully searches of the international DNA databases may well pull up some matches. Well, here is my report Inspector. Do you have any other questions?'

'Not for the moment Mr Ford. Thanks again for coming in, I do appreciate it.'

'I'll be on my way then,' he concluded, and Sally showed him out of the office.

Alex was looking pensive as Sally returned.

'What did you make of that Sally? Another coincidence? Or is it significant that the young woman in the grave came from east India; exactly where Carter spent his last overseas assignment?'

'Yes, I clocked that too.'

'Of course, we must keep an open mind for the moment and shouldn't forget there were other people working on that project. We need to find out who else was there and if possible, speak to them as a matter of urgency. We now know for certain that Professor Leonard Larkin was working as a Field Assistant, and I intend to visit him myself tomorrow. Even if none of the others on site was involved in the actual death, they may have seen something that could give us a clue as to what happened, and when. If that trench was already opened, someone may have noticed its appearance change at some point. Maybe it wasn't so deep? We need to find out from the University, who else, apart from Professor Larkin would have been working on that project.

Chapter 19

Alex arrived home that afternoon to an empty house, the children not yet back from school. She knew Dave wouldn't be home for a couple of hours at least. She parked the car in the garage to leave room on the drive for Dave's car when he finally arrived. She opened the front door and stepped into her refuge from the world outside.

It felt good to have the place to herself for once and made herself a cup of tea. Carrying it upstairs, she ran a hot bath. Sipping her tea, she luxuriated in the warm water as she began to unwind. She hadn't realised just how stressed she had been feeling. Not surprising, she told herself. The last week had been hell if she were honest, the intense physical pain of the raw grief she was going through never went away. The worst part of grieving, she observed as she lay there, is the finality of it. No going back. No chance to say, 'I love you'. The yearning for one more hug. It was horrendous and of course she was grieving not just one parent, but two, and her anger at her father still rumbled on even though she tried to supress it.

Being involved in her work allowed her, for brief moments, here and there, to push it aside, but always it returned with a vengeance whenever she let her guard down. And now it was truly down. As she relaxed, she allowed herself the luxury of letting go of her grief and tears poured down her cheeks as she called out to her mum and dad in an agony of loss.

Gradually she began to feel calmer and more able to bear it. Finally, she shivered, realising the water was getting cold and as she stepped out onto the bathmat she heard the front door slam, followed by the clatter of shoes and bags being discarded in the hallway. The children were home, and it was time once again to put her grief aside and attend to the needs of her family.

She knew that they were also grieving and would need her support to come to terms with their own feelings of loss. In the meantime, along with Dave, she needed to maintain the family's equilibrium. Life goes on, she heard her mother saying, as she had heard her say so many times in her life. Dressing quickly in a tracksuit she went down to the kitchen to find Johnny and Aby raiding the fridge.

'Hi mum!' Johnny exclaimed, 'I didn't know you were home!'

'Clearly not,' Alex quipped with a smile. 'Don't spoil your appetite, supper'll be early tonight. In fact, it will be on the table as soon as Dad gets home.'

'What're we having mum?' Aby asked, then without waiting for an answer, added hopefully, 'Can we have chips with it?'

'No, I'm afraid not Aby, we're having a good old spagbol and rice! No chips. Anyway,' she went on, 'haven't you two got some homework to do?'

'Oh mum!' they chorused, then Johnny spoke, 'I haven't got much, I think I'll do it later.'

'Oh no you don't Johnny Scott, you'll do it now and feel much better for getting it off your mind. Go on, off you go. You too Aby. Then we can all relax together after supper without having to worry about it.'

'Okay!' Aby droned and dragged herself off reluctantly to get on with it.

Alex started preparing the meat sauce for the spagbol and then poured herself a glass of wine. It had become a bit of a habit, a glass before supper. It just helped her to relax a little and seemed to give her an appetite.

With a smile she heard Dave opening the front door and was glad that for once the whole family would be able to eat together. They needed that, she thought to herself, and proceeded to place the plates in the warming drawer and the pan of water on the hob, ready for the spaghetti.

However, her smile faded as she saw the worried expression on her husband's face.

'What on earth's the matter?' she asked.

'Not good news I'm afraid love,' he replied.

'Why? What's happened?'

'You know we had a financial audit a few weeks ago?'

'Yes, but you said you thought it had gone pretty well.'

'I did, and I was confident the report would be a good one.'

'And?'

'And it wasn't. It was terrible. They found some discrepancies in the accounts! That's never happened before, and of course, the buck stops with me.'

'What do you mean, it stops with you?' Alex queried. That sounds ominous, she thought.

'Well, obviously there will be an investigation, and they'll expect answers. As District Manager, they'll expect me to have them.'

'Have you any ideas as to how the discrepancies have arisen?'

'Not yet, but obviously I will have to look into it in detail, and fast.'

'I know you'll do your best love, but of course, it is worrying for you.'

'It certainly is, and the worst of it is, to be honest, at this moment I have no idea where to start.'

'To start what?' Johnny piped up as he walked into the kitchen.

Dave glanced at Alex with a slight shake of his head to cut off any further conversation, not wishing to enter into a discussion with his son about how he should be doing his job.

'Nothing that need concern you Johnny,' he told him. 'Homework finished then?'

'Yep, I didn't have much today, just a bit of revision for a chemistry test.'

The family meal turned out to be rather a tense one after all. Not as enjoyable as Alex had hoped. Dave was understandably distracted, and Alex short on patience when dealing with the constant bickering of the children. In fact, everyone seemed relieved when it was over. Johnny and Aby disappeared back to their rooms to escape into their gaming worlds, Dave went off into the lounge to pour himself a large scotch and Alex was left to clear up the debris of the meal; unfortunately, not the cosy family atmosphere she needed right now.

She found Dave on his second glass of whiskey. This wasn't like him; he rarely drank at home and never alone.

'I know it sucks love, but I'm sure you'll sort it. They do offer support, don't they?'

'Of sorts, but the buck still stops with me.'

Then remembering what Alex must be going through, he went on,

'Anyway, enough of my problems, how are you?'

'I'll be glad when the inquest and the funerals are over. I know I'll never really get over it but at least we'll get some closure of sorts then. But you know, one of the worst things is that I feel so angry at Dad. How could he have been so careless, pulling out into traffic like that?'

'Poor love, it's inevitable that you will feel like that for a while. Come here,' Dave said gently, patting the cushion beside him on the sofa.

As she sat down, he put his arm around her and held her close as she placed her head on his shoulder. Finally, this was just what she needed, to feel loved and secure in her husband's arms. No need for words, just mutual love, and support. She realised once again how lucky she'd been in her choice of life partner.

Chapter 20

Alex had rung Professor Larkin's office by eight-thirty the following morning. Initially, his secretary, sounded rather officious, saying his diary was full for the day. However, when Alex explained who she was, and that she was conducting an enquiry relating to a project he had been involved in at Old St Paul's Church, Little Stretford, some years earlier, Miss Lowe agreed to ask the Professor if he was able to make time to speak to her.

His secretary having explained who was calling and what it concerned, she put Alex through to him and he immediately answered,

'DI Scott, I'm not sure how I can help you. That project was years ago, and I don't remember much about it.'

'I understand Professor. None the less, talking it through with me may jog your memory, and often the smallest details can be very helpful in a case like this.'

'What exactly is the case about Inspector?' he queried.

'I'd rather not discuss it over the phone Professor. I can be with you by ten-thirty this morning, if you could make yourself available?' Alex said firmly.

'Err, well, yes, I could be. How long do you think we'll need? I have a lecture to deliver at eleven-thirty.'

'I shouldn't think it will take us more than thirty minutes,' Alex replied.

'Very well then, I'll look forward to seeing you at ten-thirty.'

'Thank you Professor. Until later then.'

By ten-twenty, Alex was sitting outside his office, wondering if this interview was likely to reveal any clues about what had happened at the site all those years ago. She knew it was a long shot, but from experience, she also knew that, when prompted, people often unexpectedly remembered events and even feelings long forgotten.

At precisely ten-thirty, the phone on the secretary's desk rang and after answering it with a brief,

'Very well sir,' she turned to Alex saying, 'The Professor will see you now Inspector.'

Feeling rather as though she was being summoned into the headmaster's room to be punished for some misdemeanour, Alex thanked her, then stood up and opened the door to the Professor's office.

Behind a large desk sat a rather diminutive elderly gentleman. Alex thought to herself, if she had been asked to describe her idea of a Professor of Anthropology, he would be the embodiment of it. He was, she guessed, around sixty years old, with grey hair, or what was left of it. Just a few whisps here and there covered his pate, with tufts of rather unruly locks forming a fringe around the sides and back of his head. His half spectacles were perched precariously on the end of his nose. As she entered, he looked up sharply, as though surprised at being disturbed,

'Ah, good morning, Inspector, do sit down.'

'Thank you, Professor,' Alex replied, 'and thank you for seeing me'.

'So, what is this all about Inspector? It all sounded very mysterious over the phone.'

'There is certainly a good deal of mystery about it. Would you mind answering a few questions?'

Peering over his spectacles, he replied,

'I'll do my best, of course, but as I said, it's a long time ago and although I've tried since you rang, I can't recall much at all about that particular project.'

'First of all, Professor, you will remember I'm sure, that the project was run by Professor Robert Carter?'

'Yes, I do.'

'And do you recall that, as well as excavating around the site of the main building and the cloister walls, a further trench was opened up on the site?'

'I do remember that, yes.'

'Good, well, can you recall whether anything of archaeological interest was discovered in that trench?'

'As it happens, I worked on it myself, and we didn't discover much of interest, just a few fragments of iron-age pottery.'

'Is there anything odd about that trench that sticks in your mind?'

'What do you mean Inspector?'

'For instance, who made the decision to close it up?'

'As project manager, it would have been Professor Carter.'

'And was that a surprise to you? Did you feel it was being closed up prematurely?'

'Well, thinking about it now, that does stick in my mind because it was unusual. I do remember feeling that we hadn't explored it as thoroughly as I would have expected, but of course, I deferred to the Professor, who had much more experience than myself at the time.'

'So, if I was to tell you that during the current excavation, a significant find has been located just over three feet below the surface, what would be your reaction?'

'I would be astonished. I can't remember exactly what depth I excavated it to, but from experience, it would have been at least four feet, probably more, depending on the site and soil conditions. A final depth of three feet would have been very unusual to say the least.'

'And who actually filled in the trench? Was it one or more of the students?'

'Yes, it would have been. I wouldn't normally have been involved in backfilling the trench.'

'So, am I right in assuming you wouldn't have scrutinised the trench itself before it was re-filled with earth and therefore not have noticed that it looked rather shallower than when you had finished excavating it?'

Looking rather puzzled he confirmed that was indeed the case.

'Thank you, Professor, that's very helpful.

'Can't you tell me what this is all about Inspector?'

'Unfortunately, Professor, as this is very much a live investigation, I'm not at liberty to give you that information at the moment.'

At this point, the Professor pointedly peered through his glasses at his wristwatch, and Alex got the distinct impression that she was being dismissed. As she had already posed all the questions she needed to, she brought the meeting to a close saying.

'Well, thank you Professor, I think that's all for now. I may need to speak with you again though, as things develop.'

'Of course, Inspector, just give my secretary a ring to make an appointment. I do have a rather busy schedule, so I leave it to Miss Lowe to deal with all that.'

Alex stood up and offered her hand to him over the desk,

'Thank you for seeing me Professor.'

'No problem, although I can't imagine I've been much help.'

'Oh, you have, I assure you, and thank you once again,' Alex replied as she turned and left.

As she was driving back to the office, Alex went over the conversation she had just had with the Professor. So, he did recall a trench had been filled in rather prematurely, in his opinion, and that decision would have been made by Robert Carter. He also commented that he would have expected it to be deeper than three feet, indicating that there could have been space to deposit the body and cover it with earth before telling his team to close up the trench.

All in all, Alex felt that the interview had been very useful, reinforcing the likelihood that Carter had been involved in the murder, if that is what it turned out to be. As to that, Hilary may well have evidence to share with them by now, and Alex decided to call the forensics lab, before returning to her office.

Chapter 21

After parking up outside the station, Alex called Hilary to see if she had any news. Hilary said that she had now brought all the remains back to the lab and had some idea as to how the woman had died. Hilary answered, saying,

'Can you pop over to the lab, Alex? I'd like to talk it through with you.'

'Sure Hilary, I'll come over right away.'

The forensics lab was in a separate building next to the police station itself, and Alex hurried over, eager to listen to what Hilary had to say.

When she entered the lab, it was rather a shock to see the bones from the grave laid out full length on a slab, its skull and forearm now back where they belonged. Seeing the complete skeleton somehow made it seem more like a real person, less of an object to be studied.

'Ah, Alex,' Hilary began, 'I'm glad you could come over. I haven't written up my report yet, but there are a couple of things I wanted to share with you.'

'Hello Hillary, anything you can give us will be very welcome. We have precious little to go on right now. Plenty of mysteries but few solutions.'

'OK, let's see if we can help to solve one or two. First of all, the cause of death appears to be strangulation, as you can see from the fracture of the hyoid bone,' Hilary went on, pointing to a small bone at the front of the neck area of the skeleton which was obviously broken. 'This fracture occurs in around fifty percent of cases of strangulation. So, given the circumstances of the burial, probably not natural causes, or an accident.

'OK, most likely we're dealing with a murder then. We had kind of arrived at that conclusion, but it's good to have your confirmation.'

'Secondly,' Hilary continued, 'this young woman had not been living in the UK prior to her death. She had lived all her life in India, probably in the east, around Dhaka or Kolkata, previously Calcutta of course.'

'That supports the DNA evidence of a connection to possible siblings in India then. What about effects found with the body? Any clues there?'

'Well, apart from the earring and the blanket, which you already know about, there was nothing. Before being wrapped in the blanket and buried, it had been completely stripped. No clothes or shoes, nothing on the remains themselves.

'Mmm... presumably the body was stripped to reduce the possibility of identification, should it be discovered at some point. DNA was in its infancy back then, so whoever put her there probably wouldn't be aware that one day such analysis could be used to identify her, or them, for that matter.'

'Quite,' Hilary agreed. 'We are just beginning a detailed investigation of the blanket, but at first glance it hasn't revealed much. No obvious blood or other stains.'

'In your opinion,' Alex asked, 'did the death occur at the site?'

'Difficult to say, unless the blanket reveals something. If it had been used to transport her body from somewhere else, it may show up in our analysis and that should be complete in a couple of days.'

'OK Hilary, well, I'd better get up to the office, I need to check on progress.'

After pausing at the coffee machine outside the main office to get herself a cappuccino she walked into the office. Sally stepped up,

'A couple of things have come up this morning Boss. Shall I fill you in before this afternoon's briefing?'

'Sure Sally, just let me drink this coffee and have a bite to eat and I'll be all yours. Give me half an hour.'

Taking out the sandwich she'd bought for her lunch she sat down behind her desk to eat it and drink her coffee. She made notes about the meeting with Professor Larkin in her notebook and the things Hilary had just told her. Then glancing at her watch, decided Dave would probably be on his lunch break, and gave him a call.

'Hi love, to what do I owe this unexpected pleasure?' he said, sarcastically.

'Am I not allowed to ring my handsome husband?' she countered.

'Any time at all. I'm always at your disposal.'

'I just wanted to see how you're feeling about ... you know. I didn't get a chance to mention it this morning.'

'Oh, I guess I'll take it in my stride as usual. I've got a meeting today with the office managers to throw some ideas around. Oh, I rang the coroner's office by the way, to find out where they're up to. If it's fairly straightforward the inquest will probably be held fairly quickly. Once that's over we'll get the death certificates and can go ahead with the funerals.

'Oh! So how soon do you think??'

'Well, I'll ring them again in a day or two if we don't hear anything.'

'OK love,' Alex agreed.

'Anyway, what time do you think you'll be home tonight?' Dave went on, 'I'm going to be pretty late; I have a feeling this meeting may go on for some time.'

'Not too late hopefully.'

'I'll do my best, see you later,' he said, adding, 'love you!' before hanging up.

As Alex was signing off to Dave, she gestured to Sally to take a seat, then began to update her on Hilary's findings,

'I've just been over to the lab, and evidence is pointing to strangulation as the cause of death, but I'll go into more detail at the briefing shortly.'

'Does Hilary think the death occurred at the site?'

'She can't say at the moment but hopes that a detailed investigation of the blanket may reveal whether the body had been taken there from somewhere else after death.'

'How did you get on in Bristol?'

'Interesting, but nothing conclusive. You say you've had some developments here this morning?'

'Yes Boss, we have. We now have the identities of the siblings of the deceased. They are Vijay Singh and Anita Kumar. He is a Doctor of Psychiatry in Kolkata, so it may be possible to find out the identity of our body without too much trouble.'

'Right, can you call everyone together. It's time we tried to untangle some of this.'

'OK Boss will do,' Sally replied.

Standing in front of her team some ten minutes later, Alex began,

'Well, we've certainly got a complicated case here. I'll begin by updating you on my visit to Bristol this morning. I had a long conversation with Professor Leonard Larkin who had been a Field Assistant working on the project run by Robert Carter at the Old St Paul's Site thirty-five years ago. It appears that he had been excavating the trench where the remains were found, and remembers that he was instructed, rather prematurely to his mind, to close it up by the project manager Robert Carter. Unfortunately, he doesn't remember actually looking into the trench before it was filled in, as a student would have been tasked to carry out the work. I didn't really glean much else from Professor Larkin, so what else do we have? Sally, can you fill us in regarding the sibling matches the geneticist came up with?'

'It appears they were both living in Kolkata five years ago, when they took the DNA tests. Their names at that time were Anita Kumar and Vijay Singh. Of course, Anita is probably married and presumably her maiden name would have been Singh. I have found a Dr Vijay Singh working as a consultant in Seth Sukhal Karnani Memorial Hospital in Kolkata. It should be fairly easy to contact him.'

'Of course, given that the remains are those of a sister, it will need careful handling. I wonder if we could use someone from the local police to speak to him face to face, or alternatively we could arrange a video call. In fact, that may be preferable as we have no control over how the local police would handle it. Let me think about that one.'

'Leaving that aside for the moment,' Alex continued, 'I checked with forensics earlier and Hilary Black informed me that the most likely cause of death was strangulation. She also said that the deceased had lived all of her life (her words) in India, which means she must have died shortly after arriving here.'

Do we now have a cause of death Boss?' Neil asked.

'We do Neil. Forensics are indicating that she was strangled between thirty and forty years ago. Any more questions?'

As no one answered, Alex closed the briefing, stressing that the priority was to contact Dr Vijay Singh to arrange a video call in the hope that he would have some knowledge of the victim up until the time he'd last had contact with her.

Leaving the enquiry in capable hands for the moment, Alex then made her way home. She couldn't deny that she was finding work much harder than usual. It was difficult to concentrate and her usual coping strategy of compartmentalising everything just wasn't working. Whatever the stream of thought running through her head it always returned to Tidmouth and the prospect of the inquest and the funerals to follow.

Chapter 22

Arriving in the office the next day, Alex found her team hard at work tracking down Dr Singh. It wasn't hard to find him on the Internet. He was obviously quite well known in Indian medical circles. As a psychiatrist of some note, he had published several papers in the medical journals. However, getting hold of a private number on which to contact him, proved more difficult.

They did find an email address which looked like a personal one, and Alex decided that a short email from her, simply asking him to contact her urgently regarding a relative of his, was probably the best course to take for the moment. The nature of the conversation Alex needed to have with him must be explained to him personally, and not through his secretary or PA. She judged that if his sister had completely disappeared all those years earlier, he would be unable to resist trying to find out if Alex knew anything about her.

She thoughtfully crafted the email, wishing to spark his interest without causing him unnecessary alarm. India being five hours ahead, she calculated that it would be mid-afternoon in Kolkata, and it was possible that he would check his emails regularly during the working day. She wasn't disappointed, as an hour later the 'ping' on her phone told her she'd received an email, and she was delighted to see that it was from Dr Singh.

It read,

'Good morning DI Scott. Thank you for your email. I am intrigued to know to what you refer. Please send more details.

Best regards

Dr Vijay Singh'

Alex immediately replied,

'Good morning, Dr Singh. Thank you for responding so promptly to my email. However, the information I need to discuss with you is of a particularly sensitive nature and best-done face to face. Is it possible to arrange a video call with you? It is a matter of some urgency. Perhaps later today?

Best regards,

DI Alex Scott'

He replied immediately,

'Well, I am certainly intrigued Inspector. I could be free around seven o'clock this evening, our time, if that is convenient for yourself?

Dr Vijay Singh'

Alex replied,

'That would be excellent. I would prefer to use WhatsApp if that suits you. Please send me the number you would like me to use.

Regards,

DI Alex Scott'

With that, Dr Singh replied saying he would be ready to receive her call at seven o'clock and gave her a mobile number to use. She calculated that she needed to ring him just after lunch.

She called a team meeting to update everyone and to prepare for the conference call, which she was sure was to be key to unlocking the case. However, she realised she had precious little firm information to share with Dr Singh, who would undoubtedly want answers as to why his sister had been discovered at the bottom of a trench on an archaeological dig. In fact, as she quickly summarised, all she had was the remains, from which DNA had been retrieved and tested and shown to match his, and his sister Anita's DNA.

'Anything else?' she asked of her team gathered around her. 'It doesn't seem much, does it?'

'Well, do you intend to let him know about Robert Carter's project, with a view to finding a possible connection between them?'

'That's a good point Neil, but I think the main thing is to glean any information he may have about his sister; when did she leave India, why did she leave, when did he last hear from her? That might help us determine a connection to Robert Carter. If not, we really will be pretty clueless at the moment as to how she ended up dead and in that particular hole in the ground!'

'Will you share the cause of death with him?'

'I think I must play that by ear. As I said, first we need to extract as much information about his sister as we can, before I throw in that bombshell, as from that point it may be all he can focus on.'

She told them she was speaking to him later and she'd update everyone after that. Alex wound up the meeting, asking Sally and Neil to join her later to listen to what Dr Singh had to say.

After grabbing a bite to eat, Alex settled down in her office, making a few notes about the information she needed to glean from the conference call, then at two o'clock precisely, Neil and Sally came in, and Alex made the call.

After a few rings, Dr Singh answered.

'Good evening, DI Scott.'

'Good evening, Dr Singh. Thank you for agreeing to speak to me,' Alex answered, then went on. 'I have to let you know that this call is being recorded, as it relates to an ongoing investigation.'

'Of course, I understand,' he responded agreeably.

Alex introduced Sally and Neil, explaining that they would be listening in to the conversation and taking notes.

'So, DI Scott, what is this all about,' Dr Singh said a trifle impatiently.

'Of course, let me explain. During an investigation we are currently working on, we had cause to look for a match to a DNA profile, and yours and that of your sister Anita came up as matches.'

He took a moment to absorb that information, then an expression of realisation lit up his face.

'Was this a sibling connection by any chance?'

'It was Dr Singh. The results indicate that the DNA we have, belongs to a sibling of yourself and your sister Anita.'

He sat back and was obviously trying to work out what this meant. After a few moments, he asked,

'And the DNA you hold, where exactly has it come from?'

'Forgive me Dr Singh, but before I go into more detail, do you mind if I ask a few questions?'

'As you can imagine DI Scott, this news is very disconcerting and I must insist that first, you tell me where exactly this DNA has come from.'

'Very well Doctor, but you must prepare yourself for some difficult news.'

'Of course, DI Scott, please carry on.'

'The DNA has come from remains that have been recently discovered.'

'Remains!!' he exclaimed. Then, after a long pause he went on, 'I'm sorry, DI Scott, as you'll appreciate this has come as a huge shock. A sibling, you say?'

'Yes, a close relative, most likely a sibling. A female sibling in fact. Do you have any idea who that might be Dr Singh?'

'Yes, I do. I know exactly who this must be. It must be my sister Sunita.'

'I'm so sorry to be bringing you this news, but as you can imagine, our job is to find out exactly what happened to her, and when.'

'Of course Inspector, although I don't know how much help I can be as I haven't seen Sunita for over thirty-five years.'

Neil made a note in his notebook, thinking that at last, they had a name for the deceased. Sunita Singh, he wrote.

'I see,' Alex began, 'I appreciate this must be very difficult for you, but when exactly did you last see Sunita.'

He went on to explain that his sister Sunita had been banished from the family home when she discovered she was pregnant. Their parents were very strict and protective of the family's reputation. Consequently, they had thrown her out of the house and for many months he hadn't known where she was.

'It was very sad, and difficult for us to understand today, but then it was very different.'

'Of course,' Alex reassured him, 'and we're not here to judge Dr Singh. We just want to understand what happened to your sister after that.'

'There's not much I can tell you Inspector. She would not say who the father was, and I had no idea where she was living or how she was managing, being on her own and expecting a child.'

'Did you never see or hear from her again?' Alex asked quietly.

Dr Singh told her that after she had given birth to a baby girl, she had contacted him and begged him to help her to get to the UK. She told him that the father of her child was an Englishman, and she felt sure that if she could find him, he would help her to bring up the child.

'What could I do, she was my dear sister. I had to help her, but of course I couldn't tell my parents.'

He had given her enough money to travel to England, and to survive for a while until she could find the father of her child. He insisted that she buy a return ticket in case she was unsuccessful in her quest. That was on 10th September 1984, and he never saw or heard from her again.

'Is that why you took the DNA tests, in the hope of finding her Dr Singh?'

'It was. We waited until our dear parents had passed away and then agreed to take the tests and put the results on the Internet. That was five years ago now, but as you now know, we heard nothing, until now when you bring us this sad news.'

Neil scribbled the information down in his notebook. Now they had a date to work on.

Alex asked him if Sunita had given him any idea at all who the father was. He said that she hadn't, although he'd had his own suspicions.

'And what were they, exactly, Doctor?'

Well, she had, he suspected, a brief relationship with the only Englishman who had been around at the time. He was, he believed, an archaeologist working on the excavation of war graves.'

Sally glanced at Neil who was busy making notes. Alex was staring intently at the screen,

'And did she tell you what she had called the baby?'

'No, I'm afraid not, and to my shame, I never even asked her. So, what happens now Inspector?'

'Well, we must confirm without any shadow of doubt that the young lady whose remains were found is in fact your sister Sunita. To assist us to do that, is it possible for you to send us a photograph of her shortly before she left? We intend to carry out a facial reconstruction to compare it to the photograph you send. Once we have a positive ID and we have concluded our investigations as far as possible given the time that has elapsed, the coroner will hold an inquest.'

'Am I to take it that the death occurred some time ago then?'

'Yes, our forensics people put the date of death around thirty-five years ago. I'm so sorry, but it appears that your sister passed away soon after arriving in the UK.'

'But what about the baby? What happened to her?'

'That we don't know at the moment, but it is obviously something we are looking into.'

He said that if they were to find her, he would want to know, and Alex confirmed that if she was found she would pass on his details to her.

'I don't think we can go any further now Dr Singh.

'Please send us a photo if you can and we will try to confirm the identity of your sister as soon as possible and let you know the outcome, of course.'

'I will, certainly, and you mentioned an inquest. I would like to attend if you could let me have the details.'

'Of course, Dr Singh. In fact, I should think the coroner would invite you directly.'

'Good, well goodbye for now Inspector. I hope to hear more from you soon.'

'Indeed you will, Doctor,' Alex concluded.

After she had closed the call, she turned to Neil and Sally who were looking shocked.

'So, another possible connection to Robert Carter!' Sally exclaimed.

'Indeed!' Alex agreed, 'Everything seems to lead back to him somehow.'

Chapter 23

Before leaving that afternoon, Alex had spoken to her boss, Chief Inspector Brimley, to request his authorisation to get the facial reconstruction underway. She felt it was vital to make the positive identification of the body. It was looking very likely that it was Sunita Singh, Dr Singh's sister, but from experience, she knew that family relationships could be complicated and there could have been a sibling that he knew nothing about. The maxillofacial reconstruction department told her they would give it high priority, given the circumstances, and it should be available in about three days.

The next morning Hilary Black rang to say that detailed examination of the blanket had produced some hairs. DNA analysis had indicated that they belonged to a male, no relation to the deceased. Alex knew this was an important development as it was more than likely whoever the hairs belonged to would become their prime suspect.

She called Neil and Sally in to give them the news.

'That could be just what we've been waiting for Boss!' Sally exclaimed.

'Absolutely. Hilary is sending the results to Mr Ford for analysis and by tomorrow we will know whether it's showing up on any of the databases.'

When Alex arrived at the office the next morning she found Neil in a state of some excitement. There had been a message from Mr Ford to say that his report was ready if DI Scott would like to send someone over to collect it.

'Okay Neil, I can see you're keen, but then we all are, so please go over and pick it up right away.'

He was back within the hour and came into Alex's office with a brown envelope containing the report. Alex opened it quickly. This could be the breakthrough they needed to solve this case. However, when she read the report, it stated that no matches had been found. This was extremely disappointing. Given that all previous roads had led to Carter, she secretly hoped this would be just one more. Of course, she reasoned, it may be that his DNA was never uploaded to any of the databases. Unfortunately, he was no longer around for them to obtain his DNA profile.

She found Sally to give her the news but as she was speaking to her, one possibility did occur to her. Meera Carter was his daughter after all!

'Sally, I think we should ask Meera Carter to give us a sample for DNA analysis. If the hairs do belong to Carter, her DNA should be a partial match.'

'Of course Boss, that's a great idea. What will you tell her though?'

'Nothing I'm sure she isn't already thinking herself, but we could frame it as being necessary to rule him out of the picture.'

Over the last couple of weeks, Meera had been finding it difficult to concentrate on the project. Even though the body had been removed by the police, the trench had been left open for the moment and the forensics tent remained in position. Consequently, she was being constantly reminded of it. There was still an uneasy feel about the place, which she put down to her fears that somehow her father may have been involved.

The project itself was progressing well and would be completed on time in a couple of weeks. It had been a successful dig from the perspective of the students, and that is what it was all about after all. Josh had proved to be a good assistant supervisor, and his constant cheeriness had helped to keep morale high. She felt that she had been less than effective in that regard, troubled as she was by her own unwelcome thoughts and fears.

Pete had been kind and supportive and their relationship continued to grow, although so far, they had been unable to express openly how they were feeling. Soon this project would be over and once they were back in Bristol, they knew they would be free to move things on. In the meantime, they had to be content with secret smiles and the odd brush of hands, which only served to heighten their desires.

Meera was desperate to know whether the police were getting anywhere with their enquiries. She needed reassurance that her father had not been involved. Until then, she couldn't rest, and although she hadn't had any more nightmares, she was finding it difficult to sleep, and when she did, it was restless and shallow. She had heard nothing from them for over a week and finally could wait no longer and rang DI Scott.

'I'm sorry to bother you DI Scott,' she began apologetically, 'but I was wondering how your enquiries are going?'

'Ah Dr Carter,'

'Meera, please.'

'Yes, Meera, I was going to call you this morning. It appears from analysis that the body was deposited around the same time your father was working on the site. Also, we have found some new forensic evidence, and ideally, we would have used his DNA to exclude him from the investigation.'

'I see,' Meera interjected immediately, 'So I'm guessing as that isn't possible, you would like me to provide a sample instead?'

'That would be very helpful Meera. Can I send someone over to take it this morning?'

'Yes of course, I'll be on site all day. But is there any other news?'

Alex, not yet ready to disclose their current reasoning, answered quickly,

'Nothing definite that I can share at this time Meera, I'm sure you understand as this is still very much a live enquiry.'

'Of course Inspector, thankyou anyway.'

After Meera had closed the call, her mind was once again in a spin. She did understand that sometimes the police needed DNA analysis to remove people from their list of possible suspects. She also knew that often, it was to rule them in, and the thought that she may be about to give her own DNA to do just that filled her with foreboding. What if it was a match? How incriminating was this new evidence? She would have a word with Pete; see what he thought.

'What's the matter Meera? What's happened?'

'Pete, I was just coming to find you. I've just had a worrying conversation with DI Scott.'

'Oh yes, what had she to say? Are they any nearer finding out who our body was?'

'I don't know, she wasn't giving much away, but rather worryingly they want me to give a DNA sample!'

'I suppose that's par for the course. They'll want to rule you out if they've found DNA they can't identify.'

'Well, that's true, but it's not to rule me out, it's to rule my father out!'

'Oh, I see,' Pete replied thoughtfully.

'She said that some new evidence has come to light, and I presume she means evidence relating to the victim. It's all rather worrying to be honest Pete.'

'I can see that, Meera. But maybe she was being straight with you, and they do just want to rule him out.'

'I know. Anyway, she's sending someone over to collect a sample from me later today,' Meera went on.

'Well try not to worry, although I know that's easier said than done. Now, I was going to suggest it was time for a break. Shall I put the kettle on?'

'Thanks Pete, you're a life saver!' Meera replied, giving him one of her special smiles that always caused his pulse to quicken.

An hour later, Hillary Black's assistant Chris turned up and emerged from the church looking for Meera. He found her talking to Josh about a piece of pottery one of the students had just unearthed. Chris walked over to her and not wishing to discuss the DNA issue with everyone else around, Meera immediately suggested they go inside.

'Of course, Dr Carter. This won't take long.'

Josh gave her a questioning look, but when she ignored him, he shrugged his shoulders slightly and carried on examining the piece of pottery. Chris followed Meera into the church and pulled out a sampling kit.

'I believe DI Scott has explained why they need this sample from you Dr Carter?'

'She has, yes.'

'And are you in agreement with me taking the sample now?'

As he spoke, he took out a consent form for her to sign.

After just a moment's hesitation, Meera signed quickly then said,

'OK, let's get on with it.'

After he'd finished, she watched him drive away, thinking to herself that was that, and hopefully she would hear no more about it.

Chapter 24

Alex rang Hilary to check that Chris had successfully taken the sample from Meera and to ask her to give it priority.

'Of course Alex,' Hilary assured her.

'Thanks Hilary. It feels as though we're getting close now.'

'No problem, we should have the result within the next twenty-four hours. Do you want it to be sent over to the geneticist or is it just for the purpose of exclusion?'

'Well, yes, it is actually, but we do need it to be compared to the DNA obtained from the hair samples in order to rule out, or in for that matter, Dr Robert Carter who I think it is safe to assume is Meera Carter's father.'

'Yes, I thought so. We'll fast track it and I'm sure Mr Ford should have your answer later tomorrow.'

'Thanks Hilary,' Alex concluded and closed the call.

It was late the following afternoon when Alex received Mr Ford's call that was to completely change the course of the investigation.

'Good afternoon DI Scott,' he began. 'I have now concluded the analysis on the sample Mrs Black sent over this morning, and I think you should prepare yourself to receive news that is very surprising, to say the least, which is why I decided to ring it through right away.'

'Please carry on Mr Ford, we certainly could do with some useful news right now.'

'Well, there are two aspects to it. Firstly, the DNA from the hair samples when compared to Meera Carter's does confirm that the hair belongs to her biological father, but secondly and even more surprising, Meera Carter's DNA shows that the body in the grave is in fact her biological mother.'

Alex was silent for a moment as she absorbed this momentous news.

'Good grief Mr Ford, that really is shocking, on both counts!'

'Indeed,' he agreed. 'Anyway, I'll send my report over by email and let you have a printed copy later.'

'Thank you for giving this work priority, Mr Ford. As you can see from the results it was sorely needed.'

Alex sat for some minutes after she'd closed the call. Her mind was racing. Finally, she called Neil in and asked him to gather the team together for a briefing.

Neil stood ready to update the incident board, as she began to give them all the news.

'I just spoke to the geneticist, and he told me that the woman in the grave was in fact Dr Meera Carter's biological mother.'

Neil added the information to the board whilst the rest of the team looked on in disbelief.

'Good God!' Sally exclaimed.

'Exactly!' Alex went on, 'Also, the DNA from the hair sample is from Dr Carter's biological father, who it seems safe to assume is Professor Robert Carter.'

Neil drew another line on the board linking the hair sample information to Carter. There was another stunned silence while that sank in. The first to speak was Ida.

'So, the body belongs to Dr Carter's mother, and the hair belongs to her father?'

'Correct,' Alex agreed. 'So, Carter is now confirmed as the prime suspect in the murder of the woman in the grave. Now we need to confirm her identity beyond all doubt.'

She turned to Sally,

'Sally, have we received the photograph of Dr Vijay Singh's sister yet?'

Checking her emails, Sally said,

'Yes Boss, it's just arrived. I'll print it off now.'

'Thanks. In the meantime, let's assume that the body is Dr Singh's sister. We will confirm that once we have the facial reconstruction picture. So, we know that she had a child which her brother had assumed was the child of an English archaeologist she'd had a brief affair with, and that she came to England to try to find him. Now we can be sure that she did find him, and that the child she brought with her was Meera Carter.'

'But none of that proves that Carter murdered Meera's mother, does it?' Neil interjected. 'It only proves that he was in contact with the blanket at some point.'

'Absolutely Neil,' Alex agreed, 'and it may or may not be possible to prove one way or the other. All we can do is try to find anyone else who might have been involved. So, we need to locate as many people as possible who were working on that project, apart from Professor Larkin who I've already spoken to. Ida, could you look into that for us?

'Also, we need to find out where Carter and his wife were living at the time. If it's still standing, is anyone around who might have seen or heard something unusual? I know it's a long shot, but worth a try, I think. Neil, could you make a start on that please?'

'What about locals in and around the village? Maybe someone may remember seeing something suspicious at the time?'

'That's a good point Neil. Although there are no houses in the immediate vicinity of the church, someone may have seen suspicious goings on in the middle of the night. The pub might be a good place to start. They usually have an idea who it could be useful to speak to. Could you check that out Neil.'

'Sure thing Boss, will do,' Neil answered, rather too eagerly, which prompted a few sniggers.

'Finally,' Alex continued,' we need to look into Carter's marriage. Were he and Shaheen actually married and if so where and when? We also need to get hold of Meera Carter's birth certificate. Was it a fake? Does it state that she was born in India or England? Who is named as the mother? Who is named as her father? If her birth was registered in India, do the immigration records show when, how and with whom she was brought to the UK? Could you look at that as well Neil? Perhaps you could work with him on that Noel?' Alex added, glancing across at the young man who was sitting across the room, next to Ida.

Noel nodded and Neil replied,

'Sure thing Boss.'

Alex continued, 'Did any of their family or friends notice the sudden appearance of a child? We must assume that Carter and his wife immediately took the baby as their own. Somebody must have wondered where it had come from. Of course, all this means that they must have at least been aware of Meera's mother's death, or they wouldn't have kept her and pretended she was their own.'

'Everything is pointing to Robert Carter or his wife or both, having killed her then,' Sally said with conviction.

'That is undoubtedly true, but we owe it to the victim and of course to Meera Carter to be absolutely sure, or as sure as we can be as to how and at whose hands she met her death.'

'When will you inform Dr Carter about her mother?'

Not quite yet Sally. This is going to be traumatic for her and I'm not ready to say that either her father or the woman she has always known as her real mother, or both, are responsible for depriving her of her birth mother, and in such brutal circumstances.'

'OK Boss,' Sally replied, 'So I guess you want to wait until we have ruled out any other possibilities?'

'Correct Sally, so the sooner we can tie up the loose ends I've outlined, the sooner we can be straight with Meera Carter. I'll give the maxillofacial unit a ring to see when we can expect the facial reconstruction image to compare to the photo sent over by Dr Vijay Singh. If that's a match at least we will have a complete name, and even an image of her mother. It's the least we can do, given that her world is about to be turned on its head. Any questions?' Alex concluded, and receiving no response, closed the briefing, saying they would re-convene when the results came in from the facial re-construction, or anything else came up.

After the briefing Alex called the facial reconstruc-tion unit, who explained that their work should be con-cluded in a couple of days and that as it was needed urgently, they would forward the image to her directly by email. So, Alex was optimistic that providing the loose ends were tied up quickly, by the end of the week she may be in a position to speak to Meera Carter to give her the news about her biological mother, not a conversation she was looking forward to having, but a very necessary one, nonetheless.

Driving home that afternoon, Alex reflected on what had been revealed earlier in the DNA results. She usually managed to keep her work and private life separate but given that she was still grieving deeply for her mum and dad, it shouldn't have surprised her that thinking about telling Meera about her birth mother was bound to create resonance in her own emotions. She felt deeply sorry for Meera. She would soon be feeling that her whole life had been a lie and would have no idea who the woman she had always known as her mother was.

Eventually she would have to go through the inquest into her mother's death, something Alex herself would soon be experiencing. Of course, she mused, it would be much harder in a way for Meera as it was looking increasingly likely that she may never get justice for her mother. She may also have to understand that it was her beloved father who had killed her, as far as can be proved, given that he was no longer around.

Of course, there was another similarity between what she was going through and what Meera would soon have to face and she realised with horror that it was her own father who, by pulling out into that road, had been responsible for her own mother's death and once again she almost shouted out loud,

'Dad, why in God's name weren't you more careful!'

As soon as the words left her lips though, she felt guilty. She knew it wasn't fair to blame her father, but all the same it was difficult not to. What an utterly dreadful situation for them both, Alex pondered, as she turned into Wavertree Avenue

<h1 style="text-align:center">Chapter 25</h1>

It was late Friday afternoon when the email arrived with the picture attached. Alex quickly opened the file, and gasped as she found herself looking at the image of a young woman. The resemblance to Meera Carter was unmistakeable. She had the same slim face and high cheekbones, and as the facial reconstruction unit had been told that she was probably from South Asia, they had given her dark hair and brown skin tone, further emphasising the similarity. The photograph which Dr Singh had sent had looked vaguely like Meera Carter, but it was a blurred and somewhat faded image, making it difficult to be sure of the resemblance. The picture she was now looking at left no room for doubt in her mind. This was the woman who had given birth to Meera Carter, and she was sure that once he saw the picture Dr Singh would confirm that she was his sister Sunita.

Over the past week, Alex's team had been following up on the various tasks she'd given them and at a briefing earlier that afternoon had given her the unwelcome news that most of the lines of enquiry had drawn a blank. Neil had informed them that the street where the Carters had lived had since been replaced by a modern office block. He had visited the Crooked Gate and spoken to the landlord. They had only had the tenancy for the last ten years so had no personal recollections regarding the old church site. However, he had suggested he should speak to the two old timers who regularly played dominoes in the bar.

'I did catch up with them that evening and had a brief chat with them. They were delighted to be talking about what was apparently their favourite subject, the strange goings on up at the old church. However, they seemed more interested in telling ghost stories about the place and had no definite recollections about the events of a particular night. I don't think they could give us anything concrete Boss.'

'Ok Neil, thanks. What about the marriage?'

Neil said they hadn't been able to obtain a marriage certificate for Robert and Shaheen Carter, but it was possible they had been married in India. Also, there was no record of Meera's birth in England, but they had been able to obtain information from immigration records that a Sunita Singh had arrived with a baby girl called Anita. So, Sunita had named her daughter after her sister Anita. Another piece in the jigsaw was now firmly in place.

Ida on the other hand, had had no luck locating anyone else who had been working on the site at the time, apart from Professor Larkin, whom Alex had already ruled out.

However, with his help Sally had found a couple of people who had known the Carters socially in the late eighties, who confirmed that they had a baby called Meera, but as far as they had been told, she was their daughter, born shortly after their marriage, which they thought had taken place in Bristol.

With no further leads to follow up regarding any alternative suspects, Alex judged the time had come to speak to Meera Carter but made the decision to leave it until after the weekend. It would give her time to consider her words carefully after weighing up once again all the evidence, circumstantial as it was, before giving Meera the news. After that, she intended to speak to Chief Inspector Brimley to suggest that the case be wound up and handed over to the coroner's office for them to schedule the inquest.

Sally and Neil had both been in face-to-face contact with Meera and she showed them the reconstructed image. They both agreed that the similarity was striking. She instructed Sally to send a copy of the image to Dr Singh asking for his confirmation of the resemblance to Sunita as she was when he last saw her.

Alex continued,

'There is one other piece of this puzzle that needs to be confirmed. As far as I know, Meera Carter believes she was born in England, but the evidence suggests that she was in fact born in India as Anita Singh. Presumably, she will have a copy of her birth certificate, which we will need to check for authenticity. If we've got this right, it will be a fake. I intend to speak to Meera Carter on Monday and will ask her for the certificate, and I also feel I now must put her in the picture about her birth mother's remains.

With that, Alex wound up the briefing and half an hour later was on her way home. She hoped she would find an hour or two to go through everything in her own mind before Monday morning, but she had reluctantly decided to go down to Tidmouth on the Saturday as it had occurred to her that she needed to empty the fridge and get rid of any fresh food which may be lying around. She was annoyed with herself not to have done it when she'd visited the house to collect the paperwork but realised, she hadn't been in any fit state to deal with it then. She wondered if Dave would go with her, but what about Johnny and Aby? Should they take them? Not a good idea, she decided. In any case they wouldn't stay over and would be home by suppertime.

She spoke to Dave later that evening when the children were upstairs, and he agreed to go with her.

'The kids'll be fine here love. We can get away early and be back by late afternoon.'

Predictably, the day proved to be harrowing. Opening the fridge the shock of seeing the quiche and salad her mother had bought, presumably for their supper when they returned from the hospital appointment, tore her apart. She let out an involuntary sob and Dave drew her towards him,

'Come here love,' he whispered and then held her close until he felt her body relax.

It took them half an hour or so to empty the fridge and larder, placing everything into plastic bags before dropping them into the dustbin beside the garage. They took one last look round, Dave making sure that all the switches were turned off and the plugs taken out, before double checking the windows.

'Right love are you ready?' he asked quietly.

'For now, but I don't know when or how we're going to sort this lot out, do you?' she replied, glancing round the room at the fabric of her parents' lives, most of which was now redundant.

The sadness and futility of it all struck her with force once again, but she firmly fought back the tears as Dave assured her that everything would be taken care of in due course.

'Come on love, let's get going,' he went on, 'we need to be home by suppertime.'

Monday morning found her still unsure how to broach the subject with Meera Carter. She didn't normally have any problem imparting bad news to relatives but somehow this one was different. She knew why of course. Her own situation was amplifying her anxiety about how Meera would react when told that the bones her team had uncovered belonged to her birth mother when she had no idea that Shaheen had not given birth to her.

However, she knew it must be done, and as soon as she arrived in the office, she told Sally to contact Meera to ask her to come in. This was something she had to do face to face.

Meera was on site drafting her notes on the project which would be completed by the end of the following week when her phone rang.

'Good morning, Dr Carter,' Sally began, 'Sergeant Nugent here.'

'Good morning Sergeant. Have there been some developments?'

'DI Scott would like you to come into the office as soon as possible as she has something to discuss with you,' Sally replied.

'Oh, that sounds ominous,' Meera quipped, before continuing, 'Well I could come over after lunch, if that's alright?'

'Yes, that would be fine. We'll look forward to seeing you later. Say around one o'clock?'

'No problem. Goodbye Sergeant.'

Meera sat for a few moments, wondering what on earth DI Scott wanted to discuss with her that couldn't be dealt with over the phone. Something important, obviously. That familiar feeling of dread welled up in her stomach as her thoughts inevitably turned to her father. Had the DNA sample she'd given, far from ruling him out, ruled him in, as she had feared?

Needing to speak to Pete, her 'go to' confidante, rather than walking over to his trench and not wanting to set tongues wagging further than they already were, she sent him a text asking him to pop over for a minute.

As he came into the church he spoke quickly in a concerned tone,

'What's happened, you look terrible Meera.'

'Sergeant Nugent just rang. Oh Pete, they want me to go in this afternoon. DI Scott wants to discuss something with me.'

'Right, and does that worry you?'

'Well, I'm wondering whether that DNA sample I gave them, rather than ruling my father out, may have implicated him further. They didn't tell me what the 'new evidence' was, but what if my DNA was in fact needed to confirm his involvement?'

'Well, try not to worry. It could be something completely different. Perhaps they've come up with a question about the skeleton, which needs your technical expertise.'

'That's true, I suppose,' Meera replied grudgingly. 'But thanks Pete, it's a good job someone round here keeps a sense of proportion. Mine seems to have deserted me right now.'

'That's not really surprising, is it? With your father's connection to this site, it's bound to be emotional for you,' Pete went on, 'I wish I could do more to help you.'

Despite their tacit agreement not to let their relationship progress until they were back in Bristol, he couldn't help reaching out to her and as their hands met it was as though an electric shock ran through his body, and he was consumed with the desire to take her in his arms. He couldn't bear to see her distressed like this.

For a moment it seemed as though she was moving towards him, but then she suddenly stopped.

'Not here Pete,' she said softly, pulling her hand away.

'I know, I'm sorry Meera, but it's so hard. You know how I feel about you, don't you?'

Without waiting for an answer, he quickly went on,

'Of course, I know you're right. Anyway, I'd better be getting back outside, before they all start adding two and two together.'

'Well, thanks for your listening ear, as usual, and I really don't know how I would have coped without having you around these past weeks.'

'I wouldn't want to be anywhere else, believe me,' he assured her.

Chapter 26

Driving over to the police station, Meera was still feeling anxious, wondering once again why they insisted on talking to her there. This is ridiculous, she told herself. I've got nothing to hide or be nervous about, so why am I feeling so stressed out?

Inside the station she walked up to the reception desk, where PC Dodds was on duty.

'Can I help you?' he queried.

'Thanks, I'm here to see DI Scott.'

'I see, I'll give her a call to tell her you've arrived. What name should I say?'

'Dr Carter,' Meera told him.

'Would you like to sit down,' he said, gesturing towards a row of chairs at the back of the waiting room, 'I'm sure she'll be down shortly.'

Meera thanked him and sat down. Five minutes later, Sergeant Nugent stepped out of the lift and walked towards her, saying,

'Thanks for coming in Dr Carter. Please come this way,' and led her down a short corridor to a side room which she assumed was an interview room.

In fact, the room wasn't entirely as she expected. Used to watching crime dramas on television, she had thought it would be bare, with just the usual table and chairs. This seemed more like a small lounge, with a sofa and a couple of easy chairs, with a coffee table between them.

'DI Scott will be down shortly, but could I get you a cup of tea or coffee while you're waiting?' Sally asked her.

'Oh, a coffee would be fine; milk, no sugar, thanks,' Meera replied, rather confused at this unexpected hospitality. A few minutes later Sally returned with her coffee.

Meera had settled down on the sofa and was trying to relax when Alex arrived.

'Ah! Dr Carter! Thank you for coming in,' she began.

Eager to know why she had been summoned, Meera skipped the polite conversation, going straight to the point,

'Is it about the body? Do you have an identity?'

'First of all, Dr Carter, could I ask when you last saw your mother?'

'My mother? What has she got to do with all this?'

Meera was completely thrown by the question which seemed so utterly divorced from the events that had brought her there.

'Please, just answer the question,' Alex insisted, firmly but gently, very aware of the bombshell which was about to descend on Meera.

'Well, I last saw her in the hospital the day she died.'

'I see, and when was that?'

'It was five years ago,'

Alex and Sally exchanged glances, then Sally asked,

'And what did she die of?'

'She had breast cancer. But what has this got to do with the body in the grave?'

'Just one more question, if you don't mind. Where was she buried?'

'She wasn't, she was cremated,' Meera stated with some impatience.

After a short pause Alex said quietly,

'Forgive me for asking this, but do you believe the person you called mother was, in fact, your birth mother?'

Meera was utterly bewildered and angered by the question and immediately said, with some force,

'What kind of a question is that? Of course she was my birth mother! For God's sake, what is all this about?'

'Because,' Alex began, as gently as she could, 'DNA analysis points to the fact that.' Alex paused for a moment, 'the person buried in the grave was your birth mother.'

Meera reeled. What on earth was she saying? Her mother was cremated five years ago, how could she possibly have been buried without ceremony in an unchristian burial?

'Why? How?'

'Well as you know we took samples from the burial for forensics to carry out DNA and other tests.'

'And?' Meera said forcefully, 'Tell me what you've found.'

Alex briefly glanced at Sally before saying quietly,

'The DNA results were strong, and we compared them to the results from your own DNA test.'

'I thought you took mine to rule my father out,' Meera said with a hint of annoyance in her voice, then went on, 'and now you're telling me the DNA from the body is a match for my DNA?' Meera asked, incredulously.

'The geneticist confirmed it. You are definitely the daughter of the person in the grave. I'm so sorry to have to give you what must be devastating news Meera.'

Meera didn't respond at first. Her mind was racing, trying desperately to make sense of it all. So, if that was her mother, who the hell was the woman, Shaheen, who had been married to her father and who she had called mum all her life? And her father! Whatever had happened to her birth mother, surely her father must have known. Why hadn't he ever told her about her. And why in God's name was she buried in a trench in the dig he'd been running?

She knew of course that the police would be ahead of her on this. They'd had time to absorb the news and discuss it.

'I don't understand any of this,' Meera said at last.

'I know it's come as a terrible shock Meera, and we have been doing our best to find out exactly what happened to your mother and why.'

The fog in Meera's brain was starting to clear and she needed to know, above all else, when her mother, her real mother, as she now had to get used to saying, had actually passed away.

'Do you know when she died and was buried?'

'It appears that she died shortly after arriving in this country from India. '

'And when was that, exactly?' Meera asked.

'She arrived on the 25th September 1984.'

Meera looked utterly shocked, and took a moment before declaring,

'But how could that be? That means she must have brought me to England from India when I was only two months old!'

'That's correct,' Alex confirmed. 'We also have some other news for you, about your Indian family, if you are ready to hear it. '

Meera nodded vigorously.

'Definitely. I need to know everything if I'm to understand any of this.'

'I know all this is a lot for you to take in. Did anyone ever tell you about them?'

'No, nobody ever talked about any relatives in India, which I must admit I have wondered about over the years.'

'Well through the DNA samples we've taken from yourself and the victim, your birth mother, we have located two of your Indian relatives.'

'Where are they? Are they in England?' Meera asked with urgency in her voice.

'No, they're both in Kolkata, India. They are siblings of your birth mother. Dr Vijay Singh is your uncle, and Anita Kumar is your mother's sister.'

'Have you contacted them? What did they know about what happened to my mother? Did they tell you her name?'

Indeed, her name was Sunita. Dr Singh told us that your mother found she was pregnant, and she had to leave home because her parents believed it would bring shame on the family.'

'That's so sad! So did he say how and why she came to England?'

'Well apparently, shortly after giving birth to you, your mother contacted Vijay saying that she needed money to get to England to find your father, hoping that he would support the two of you.'

'So he helped her to come to England then?'

'He did,' Alex replied and was about to go on when Meera suddenly exclaimed,

'And do my DNA results confirm that Robert Carter is my biological father?!'

'Everything points to that fact, yes."

'Is that because of the new evidence you found? What was that, exactly?'

Alex hesitated, instinctively not wishing to share evidence, particularly with a close relative of the suspect, but in this case, she couldn't see any reason why Meera shouldn't know. After all, there would be no prosecutions, as the only suspects they had were deceased.

'Well, we found hairs wrapped inside the blanket that your DNA confirmed had come from your biological father. So, we have to assume that it was your father that Sunita was coming to see, and in fact, all the evidence suggests that she did indeed find him.'

'Then, and I can't believe I'm saying this, do you now believe that he was involved in the murder of my mother?'

'I'm afraid to say that circumstantial evidence is pointing that way. As far as we are able, we have ruled out anyone else from the dig being involved. However, it may be impossible to prove it one way or another as of course we are unable to question either your father or Shaheen.'

Meera was undoubtedly in shock and quite unable to take it all in. Finally, her mind threw up the question; who the hell was the woman who brought me up then?

Chapter 27

Struggling to comprehend what Alex had just re-vealed, that the woman she had always called mum was not her mother at all, finally, she asked,

'Who was Shaheen then; do you know?'

'Not right now, we're still looking into that. We need to see your father and Shaheen's marriage certificate as it would have her maiden name on it. Do you have a copy?'

'Well, I always understood that they were married in Kolkata, India, but I don't believe I have a copy of their marriage certificate. Look, none of this makes any sense!'

'Would you mind letting us take copies of any birth, marriage or death certificates you do have in your possession. They may help us to unravel this mystery.'

'Err... Yes, of course.'

'If you feel ready Meera, I do have one other thing to share with you. In order to confirm with Dr Vijay that the victim was his sister Sunita, we carried out a facial reconstruction, and I now have the image of the face. Are you ready to see it?'

'Oh, I'm ready alright!' Meera exclaimed.

'If you're sure,' Alex continued, then opened the folder on the desk in front of her, slowly turning it towards Meera.

As she looked down at the face before her, Meera gasped. She had seen that face before! She suddenly went weak and grabbed hold of the desk for support as she struggled to comprehend not only who this was, but also how she could have already seen it weeks ago as she had gazed on the skull Pete was carrying from the trench.

Alex was concerned but not surprised at Meera's reaction.

'This is your birth mother Meera, and as you can see you bear a strong resemblance to her.'

Meera nodded silently, as yet unable to form any words. Finally, after a minute or so she said,

'This isn't the first time I've seen that face Inspector.'

'Well, it's bound to look familiar to you Meera.'

'No, that's not what I mean! This is going to sound ridiculous, and I can't really believe it myself, but I saw this face when I first looked at the skull as it was taken from the trench.'

Alex, for once stuck for words, looked at Sally to see what she was making of what Meera had just said.

'Well, it must have been quite a moving moment, to be removing a skull from someone's grave Meera, or perhaps it was a trick of the light.'

'I said it would sound ridiculous to you, but it was real to me. I've excavated many bodies and never had a reaction like that before. And how do you explain that it was this face that I saw?'

Meera went on to tell them about all the nightmares and odd feelings she'd had over the past weeks, and Alex and Sally listened sympathetically, understanding that Meera needed to share all this with someone to help her to deal with the shock.

Finally, Meera said,

'I know this all sounds crazy to you, but to me it now makes perfect sense. Somehow, my mother has been trying to reach me since we first planted a spade in the ground above her. Well, I'm glad that at last she's free from that dreadful situation and presumably I'll be able to lay her to rest?'

'Of course. Eventually, once the coroner releases the remains.'

'Thank you. Could I have a copy of this photo please?'

'Certainly,' Alex agreed, then turned to Sally, 'Would you mind printing one off for Meera?'

'Well,' said Alex, 'I think that's all for now Meera. I know this must all have come as a dreadful shock to you. Do you have any further questions?'

'Just about my Indian relatives. Do they know about me? Do they know Sunita's body was found?

'They do, and that it is their sister, and I promised to let him know if you were found. I intend to call him immediately after this meeting. He has already asked us to let him know when the inquest is, so that he can attend. When you're ready Meera, we will of course let you have his details so that you can contact him.'

'Well, let me think about it. I've got so much to get my head around now before I'm ready to speak to him. You mentioned the inquest DI Scott. Is that what will happen next?'

'Now that we've put you in the picture and we are sure we can't pursue the case any further it will be passed to the coroner who will probably hold a brief initial hearing to release the remains in which case you would be able to proceed with the funeral. He would also schedule a full inquest. We will of course, let you know the date when we have it.'

'Thankyou DI Scott. I'll let you have the certificates as soon as I can.'

With that, Alex and Meera shook hands. Sally returned and handed her an envelope containing the copy of her mother's image, then escorted her through reception and out of the building. As she watched her go, Sally wondered at her composure after receiving such devastating news. She's obviously still in shock, Sally thought. I don't envy her having to come to terms with the probability that her father killed her mother and lied to her for the whole of her life.

After Meera had left the office, Alex rang Dr Singh.

He picked the phone up immediately,

'Good evening DI Scott. Do you have some news for me?'

'I do, and I felt it best to speak to you personally.'

'Have you found my niece?'

'We have. A DNA sample was recently taken from the archaeologist overseeing the project where your sister's remains were discovered. This was because the only other excavation carried out at the site was run by Dr Robert Carter thirty-five years ago.'

'And did you think this Robert Carter may have been the archaeologist my sister had known?'

'That did seem likely. But the reason we wanted to check the DNA of the archaeologist running the current dig, was that she is his daughter, Dr Meera Carter.'

'Good grief, so are you now thinking that Meera Carter is in fact Sunita's child?'

'Meera's DNA matches the sample we took from your sister's remains, so yes, Meera Carter is your niece.'

There was a long pause, presumably while Dr Singh tried to work out the implications of what Alex had just said.

'Dr Singh?'

'I'm sorry Inspector, I'm just trying to understand. So, Robert Carter was the archaeologist Sunita met and is the father of her baby, the man she travelled to England to find, and that the excavation which has found her has been run by her own child, Meera, who has been brought up by Robert Carter. Is that correct?'

'It is. I have just had a meeting with Meera to explain all this to her. As you can imagine it has come as a complete shock. She had no previous knowledge of what she might find at the site when she chose it for the project. She selected the site specifically because it had been excavated by her father, as a way of paying tribute to him.

'This is indeed very shocking news Inspector. I feel very sorry for her, I cannot imagine how she's feeling right now, as everything is pointing to her father having murdered her mother.'

'Well, we are still investigating the actual circumstances of your sister's death, but as he died several years ago, it may not be possible to prove beyond doubt exactly how she died and who was responsible.'

'I see. Well, thank you for telling me all this Inspector.'

'I thought you should be aware of it before Meera speaks to you. I have told her about you and your sister and said I will let her have your details when she's ready. Understandably, being in shock right now, she wisely said that she wasn't quite ready to speak to you, but I have no doubt that she will, in due course.

'One last thing Dr Singh. Would you please set down in an email the sequence of events that took place before Sunita left India, as far as you know them? We will need your statement for the case file.'

'Of course, Inspector, I'll do it right away. And thank you once again.'

Alex closed the call, reflecting on what an emotional day it had been. Delivering such shocking revelations was never easy, but with this case, it seemed harder than ever to remain detached.

Chapter 28

Meera pulled into a layby on the A351. She was in a state of shock. Switching off the ignition she began to go through what the police had just told her. The woman in the grave was her mother! She took out the photo from the envelope Sally had given her and as she looked at the face, she was gripped by a powerful sense of sadness and loss. Alone in the car she was able to allow all her feelings to come to the surface. This young woman, younger even that she was now, had had her life snuffed out, leaving her behind, and in the privacy of the car she let her guard down and her emotions out and let the tears flow.

Afterwards she thought again about all the strange feelings and nightmares she'd been having, and uppermost in her mind was that face. The one that had appeared momentarily when she'd first looked at the skull! At first, she had thought it was her own face. Now she knew it was in fact this face, the one she was looking at, her mother's face.

Had her mother been trying to communicate with her from the moment Adam had sunk his spade into the ground on that first day? She thought about the skeleton in her dreams. On each occasion it had reached out its hands to her, pleading for her to take hold of them. She had never believed in the supernatural, but knowing what she now did, she was becoming more and more convinced that her mother had been reaching out to her, desperate to be discovered.

Now her thoughts turned to her father and Shaheen, the person she had always believed was her mother. What was their story?

Searching for some reality, she took out her phone and scrolled through the photos. There were several of family meals out, celebrating birthdays and the like. One had always been her favourite. It was of her father and herself at her twenty-first birthday dinner with her parents. He'd booked a table at a particularly expensive restaurant in London, and she remembered feeling particularly sophisticated in the tight-fitting emerald-green satin dress bought specially for the occasion. He looked handsome in his immaculate dinner suit. They both looked happy, relaxed and, yes, proud. Proud of themselves, able to enjoy such luxury, and of each other. The idea that her father could have caused anyone's death was just unimaginable to her. He always seemed such a kind and gentle man.

Then the memory of her final nightmare intruded on her thoughts. Could it be that she had witnessed what had happened? Had they argued and had he pushed her, maybe not meaning to harm her, but accidentally causing her death? She felt sick. Her father had been her rock, her guide, her motivator, and chief educator. The direction her life had taken up to now had been influenced by her desire to please him. Now she knew it had all been based on a terrible secret. Everything had changed the moment she realised the truth and she knew nothing in her life would ever be the same again.

Her thoughts turned to the dig. What on earth was she going to do about that. She knew she could not go back there. It was impossible from every angle. Professionally it wouldn't be right, now that she knew she had an intimate connection to the deceased. Emotionally it would be impossible to remain detached from what was happening on site; and yet, it was her own project. It would have to be completed for the sake of the students. As her senior site assistant, could she ask Josh to finalise the dig? She would have to explain why she couldn't carry on with it. He would expect her to have good reason, but how much could she tell him? It was a drastic step, to leave a project before it was finished. But she was convinced it was the only logical thing to do.

Taking out her phone she glanced at the time. It was almost two-thrty. She decided she needed to speak to Pete but didn't want to tell him about all this over the phone, and that she wouldn't be returning to the dig. She needed to speak to him face to face but away from the others. He was the only one who knew what she'd been going through. He would understand how she felt and maybe would be able to help her to decide how to handle all this.

Perhaps he could meet her at the Crooked Gate? The others might think it rather odd, but they already thought there was something going on between them, so would probably assume it was some kind of romantic liaison. Of course, Pete may also think that too, she thought. Oh well, I hope he won't be too disappointed.

She rang his mobile and he answered right away.

'Meera, hi,' he said, sounding surprised.

'Hi Pete. Look, something's come up and I need to speak to you, but not there. Can you meet me down at the Crooked Gate in fifteen minutes? Just tell Josh that I've asked you to meet me as I have something to discuss with you.'

Pete was thrown for a moment. Is she asking me out for a date or something, he thought, then, no, surely not in the middle of the afternoon?

'Err yes, of course Meera. See you soon then.'

He went over to Josh to explain that Meera wanted to see him down at the Crooked Gate and he'd be gone for an hour or so.

'Oh yes!' Josh declared in his usual knowing tone, 'Will that be long enough?'

'Very funny,' Pete mumbled, then strode off to get in his car.

Ten minutes later he was at the bar ordering a drink when Meera stepped through the door.

'What can I get you?' Pete asked her.

'Hi Pete, well, after what I've just been through, something a bit stronger than fruit juice. Can you make it a glass of house white please.'

'Sure thing,' Pete replied.

Meera glanced around the bar and was relieved to see it was virtually empty. While Pete was getting the drinks she chose to sit down at a table in an alcove on the far side of the bar.

'Meera, you look awful!' Pete said as he placed the drinks on the table and sat down opposite her.

'I feel awful, to be honest Pete. That was quite a session with the police this morning.'

'Why? What happened? I assume it was about the body and possible connection to your father?'

'In a way, but Pete, it was much worse than that.'

'What do you mean?'

Meera took a long drink of wine before launching into,

'I hardly know where to begin. They have had the DNA results in.'

'And did they find a match?'

'They did. And, oh God Pete! It's me!'

'You!? What on earth do you mean Meera?'

'It's very simple, but not what I would ever have imagined in my wildest dreams, and I've had plenty of those lately, as you know! The body in the grave is ... my birth mother!'

'What! How?'

'Well, the geneticist is certain that I am the daughter of the person in the grave.'

'How on earth can that be Meera? When did your mother die?'

'The woman I'd always known as my mother died five years ago, and before you ask, she was cremated. So, it seems she wasn't my real mother after all!'

'And neither she nor your father ever mentioned what had happened to your birth mother?'

'They did not. And it turns out that my real mother, who I now know was Sunita Singh gave birth to me in India, after a brief relationship with my father apparently, and when I was only a few weeks old she brought me to England to find my father to ask him for help. Her family had thrown her out, you see.'

All this had tumbled out of Meera's mouth as though she couldn't risk not getting it all out before her emotions took over once more.

'Good God! But wait a minute Meera, how on earth did she end up in an unmarked grave in the middle of Somerset?'

'That's exactly what I've been asking myself for the last hour, and I don't like the direction my thoughts are taking me, and the police are apparently thinking the same.'

'Oh Meera, I'm so sorry, all this must have come as a horrible shock,' Pete said, wishing he could take her in his arms to offer her some comfort. Of course, he knew that was impossible right now, but could he dare to hope that one day...?

'Of course, but regardless of all that,' Meera went on, 'surely, I can't continue to work on the dig. It's just not possible either professionally or emotionally. So, and this is why I wanted to speak to you. You know how this whole thing has been affecting me, what with the nightmares and everything, and I know you've felt things too. I just don't know how to handle it. Do I just shut down the project and tell everyone to leave, which seems a pity for the students. It's so important for them to complete it as they start on their final year.'

'I can see your problem Meera. Couldn't Josh take it over? We've almost finished anyway.'

'Well, he could do, but I'm not too keen to tell him about my father's involvement at this stage. Neither I nor the police have conclusive evidence, even though everything is pointing in that direction.'

'Well, couldn't you say that you're unwell?' After all, if you were sick, someone would have to take over.'

'I could, but I hate deceiving anyone, particularly colleagues who I know well. On the other hand, I don't particularly want all this talked about.'

'Well maybe it would be best in that case if you were to take Josh at least, into your confidence. I know he's a bit of a joker, but he's one of the good guys. I'm sure if you asked him, he'd understand and respect your wish not to divulge it to anyone else, for the moment at least.'

'I could do that, but I still couldn't work on the site. I'll have to go back to Bristol, and it would be difficult to do that without speaking to the University to explain why.'

'Well, I don't see what else you can do, other than to take a couple of weeks sick leave, which you could legitimately put down to stress. After all, I can't think of anything more stressful than what you're going through right now. But you could confide in Josh, to explain why you're actually having to leave the dig. I'm sure you'll find him supportive and willing to take up the responsibility of finishing the project.'

'OK Pete, that sounds like a plan. I don't want to go back to the site at all though. Perhaps you could ask him to meet me here this afternoon so that I can explain everything to him in private.'

'Of course! So, what will you do now then Meera?'

'I'll go back to my flat in Bristol and await further developments. DI Scott wants copies of my birth certificate, and anything else I have that might be useful, so I need to drop them over to the station before I do anything else.'

'Can I look you up when we've finished here Meera?' Pete asked with a slight catch in his voice.

Meera looked up at him, having noticed that he sounded a little emotional. After a moment, she smiled, saying

'That would be nice Pete. I'm going to need a good friend, and I think that's what you've become to me.'

He reached across now and placed his hand on hers, squeezing it gently.

'I'd better get back now, but I'll see you soon, in Bristol.'

'Absolutely,' she replied, then added, 'Please ask Josh to pop down then if you would. I'll be getting my stuff together. And would you ask him to bring my laptop with him?'

'Will do Meera, and if ever you need someone to talk to about all this, or anything else for that matter, you have my number.'

'I do, and thanks Pete, you've been a great help.'

'Bye for now then,' he replied in a concerned and loving tone, 'see you soon.'

Chapter 29

It was around six by the time Meera parked up in front of her apartment building in Ashley Grove. She was feeling relieved that Josh had agreed to take over winding up the dig. He had of course been as shocked as Pete to hear about her connection to the body and understood perfectly why she couldn't carry on with it herself. He had assured her he would be discreet as to her reasons for not continuing with it. But, as he pointed out, there was no guarantee the information wouldn't be made public, either accidentally or by design by the police, during their investigation. She was well aware of that she told him, but she personally needed time to think it all through before having to confront any questions that might be thrown in her direction. People were bound to be curious. Anyone would be, given the circumstances.

Now, opening the door to her apartment, it felt good to be home. A place of safety, away from scrutiny. Her own private world. She kicked off her shoes and made herself a cup of tea. She couldn't eat yet. She was still too stressed.

Being as eager as the police were to see her birth certificate and any others she could find, she climbed up on the kitchen steps to reach the top cupboard where she kept the box containing important personal papers. Taking it down she carried it into the living room before settling down to explore its contents while drinking her tea.

First, she located her own birth certificate. Her father, it stated, was Robert Carter, and her mother, Shaheen Carter. Her place of birth was given as Bristol. But how could this be? She now knew that Shaheen was not her birth mother. How could that name be on her birth certificate? Surely that should have been Sunita's name. She also now knew that she had been born, not in Bristol, but in India. This certificate must be a forgery, she realised. This piece of paper that she'd used to obtain her passport and to prove her identity many times was a total fabrication! It seemed like the very foundations of her life were crumbling beneath her.

She sat staring at the birth certificate in front of her. She was angry and felt betrayed all over again. She felt a strong urge to rip the thing up. Instead, she went back into the kitchen, opened one of the wall cupboards and took out a half bottle of whiskey. She hardly ever drank alcohol but right now she needed something to dull her emotions which were running riot. She poured herself half a glass, topping it up with water, and took a large gulp.

Forcing herself to continue to search through the papers, she found her father's birth certificate. He was born in Middlesex as he'd always told her. She didn't remember ever meeting her grandparents, who she could see were Arthur and Muriel Carter. Her father had always told her that they both died when she was tiny. Knowing what she now did, she wondered if even that was a lie. Given what she suspected he was guilty of, and unable to explain her own appearance, maybe to cover his tracks he'd had to distance himself from his own family. There was no birth certificate for Shaheen. So, she was no nearer knowing who the woman she had always known as her mother really was or where she had originally come from. Searching further, she found their death certificates which she assumed the police would also need, if only to prove they were both dead. She couldn't even face looking at them, quickly folding them up along with the two birth certificates and placing them in an envelope, ready to hand over to the police the next day.

After finishing the whiskey, she allowed herself to think about Pete. He had been so helpful and supportive, and he was very obviously attracted to her. She had to admit a warm feeling welled up inside her whenever her thoughts rested on him. She hadn't really felt anything like it before and wasn't too sure what it was. Was this love, or was it gratitude? There was so much going on in her mind right now, she really had no idea which. She realised she would have to be careful. The last thing she would want to do would be to lead him on when she knew how he felt about her. He had been so kind and supportive; she couldn't bear the thought of hurting him.

Finally, the emotional upheaval she had suffered that day caught up with her, and she closed her eyes and dozed off. She woke with a start as a car backfired on the road outside. She picked up the picture DI Scott had given her of her mother and as she looked at it couldn't help wondering what kind of a mother she would have been. She knew the picture was only an approximation of what she might have looked like, but even so, it was a kind face and very familiar given the likeness to herself.

Later, as she lay in bed waiting for sleep, her thoughts kept drifting to her father. She had lost him once when he died, and now she realised had lost him all over again. She would never be able to think fondly of him or indulge in pleasant memories of her childhood. She would have to completely close the pages of that particular book. Of course, archaeology, which had been so much of a part of their life together, would be a constant reminder. Would it still hold the same fascination for her? She doubted it. After all, she now realised, her efforts to make a success of her career had all been for him, to make him proud of her. She felt as though she had no past, and now, no future either.

She would only be able to imagine what life might have been like with Sunita. Of course, soon she hoped to meet her Indian family which would help her in that respect. At least they would be able to tell her about her mother. Would she feel some kind of bond with them? Not easy, she thought, when she'd never met them before. Well, however that turned out, she was sure they would be a part of her future which she now understood was going to be very different from the one she had always planned and worked so hard for.

Eventually she drifted off to sleep, full of imaginings of what that future might hold for her and in spite of what she'd gone through that day, slept soundly and awoke refreshed. As she ate her breakfast at the kitchen table, she remembered her musings of the night before. Could she actually give up everything she'd worked so hard for and leave archaeology behind her? Not the time to be making such important decisions, she told herself. Better to let that one lie for a while until she was sure what she really wanted to do.

Her phone rang. It was Pete.

'Meera, how are you doing?'

'Hi Pete,' she replied, 'I'm OK. Still shocked of course, but I looked at my birth certificate last night and it's obviously a total fabrication, which I had already realised it must be, but the actual sight of it still shocked me to the core.'

'God, of course, it must have done. Birth certificates are important parts of our identities, aren't they?'

'They are, and to be honest I just feel like the foundations of my life so far are crumbling away. Like I have no past and now no future.'

'What do you mean, no future, Meera?' Pete responded in an anxious tone.

'Don't worry, I'm not suicidal or anything. It's just that I don't even know if I can carry on with my archaeology career. It's so tied up with my relationship with my father and now that, in my own mind, I'm sure what he did, either by accident or design, I feel that I don't want anything more to do with him, his memory, or even archaeology itself.'

'That's understandable I guess, but what a waste of all that hard work, Meera.'

'That's not the only waste though Pete. What about all the love and respect I gave him over the years. That now turns out to have been a total waste. He didn't deserve any of it, did he?'

'It's understandable that you should feel that way now Meera, but maybe it's not the best time to be making decisions about your future.'

'I know Pete, and don't worry, I won't do anything rash.'

'Well, you know where I am if you want someone to talk to.'

'I do Pete, and I'm grateful, believe me. You've been wonderful over the last few weeks.'

As soon as she'd spoken, she regretted using the word 'wonderful' in case he misunderstood her meaning. She wasn't ready to move the relationship on yet. Her emotions were all over the place and she couldn't be sure what she felt about him right now.

'Meera, I'll always be here for you, you must know that,' his voice thick with emotion.

Unable to respond in like manner, she quickly said,

'Thanks Pete,' which was followed by an awkward silence until she went on,

'Well, I've got to go now, I have to take the certificates over to the police.'

With a slightly bewildered tone Pete said,

'Oh, err... OK Meera. I'll be back in Bristol at the weekend, can we perhaps meet up for a drink?'

'Yes of course,' she replied. 'Ring me when you get back and we'll arrange something.'

'Of course I will. Bye for now,' he said softly.

Chapter 30

As Meera prepared to take the certificates to DI Scott, for some reason, she decided to check them again before putting the envelope in her handbag. She looked at her father's birth certificate and in spite of everything, felt a pang of loss. If only she hadn't decided to use the Old Saint Paul's church site for her project! None of this would have happened and she would still have her old life and fond memories of a happy childhood.

Naturally, she was aware that it had all been founded on a grave secret. It felt as though every word her father had ever spoken to her had been a lie. If she hadn't been so keen to impress him, she may not have become an archaeologist in the first place, and in any case may not have chosen to work on the site that he had previously dug. What a supreme irony it was, that her regard for him had led her to the very spot where he'd buried her mother all those years ago.

Her mother! Well, she had found her now and would not wish it any other way. All she wanted to do was to be able to lay her to rest properly and hopefully begin to build a new life as the person she was always meant to be.

She called the police station and spoke to Sergeant Nugent to say she was coming over with the certificates and would like a word with DI Scott if she was available.

'Yes, she is here this morning Dr Carter,' Sally told her. 'What time do you think you'll arrive?'

'In about half an hour,' Meera told her.

'That's fine, I'll let her know you're on your way.'

An hour later Meera sat across from Alex in the interview room.

'Thank you for coming over so promptly Meera. We are keen to get these last few loose ends tied up and these certificates may help us to do that. Would you like a cup of tea or something?'

'No thanks, I'm fine,' Meera answered. 'To be honest, I did want a word with you anyway.'

'Yes, Sergeant Nugent told me. So what can I do for you?'

'Well, if you remember I told you that I'd had several nightmares since we began the excavation?

'Yes, I do.'

'Well, in the last one he was standing in the ruins of Old St Paul's church arguing with a woman who had her back to me, so I couldn't see who it was. As I watched he pushed the woman who fell backwards, banging her head on the ground and causing her death. Since finding out about my mother, I've kind of assumed that somehow, I had witnessed what had actually happened and that he hadn't meant to kill her; that it was really an accident.'

Alex had been sitting quietly, listening to Meera, trying not to let her scepticism show. Meera paused, then went on,

'Well, in your opinion, is this how it could have happened?'

Alex sat for a moment, wondering how much she ought to disclose to Meera before the coroner had been able to reach a conclusion about how Sunita had met her death. Eventually she began,

'Well Meera, it will of course be up to the coroner to determine the cause of death. We will just present the facts as we've been able to determine them.'

'Yes, of course, I know that. But surely you must have come to some conclusions yourselves?'

'We have Meera, but it's probably not what you want to hear.'

'Please DI Scott, I need to know. I have very few certainties left in my life now, and I must begin to rebuild it, but this time it has to be built on truth, however painful. There have been enough lies. So please, tell me what you've found out.'

'If you're sure then.'

Meera nodded and Alex went on,

'From the forensic examination it appears that the most likely cause of death was strangulation.'

Meera sat for a moment, absorbing what Alex had just said.

'So, it was deliberate then,' she said quietly.

'It appears so, as far as we can tell. I'm so sorry Meera. Of course, we may never be able to prove who actually killed her.'

'I don't need you to do that DI Scott. As far as I'm concerned it was him – I don't even want to say his name or what he was to me. He's dead and gone to me now, along with my old life.'

Meera handed over the envelope to Alex saying,

'The only certificates I have are my birth certificate and his, and both of their death certificates. As you will see my birth certificate is a complete fabrication, stating my place of birth as Bristol and my mother's name as Shaheen.'

Alex had taken the certificates out and was looking at them one by one.

'Yes, so I see Meera. Of course, we now know you were born in India.'

'Quite. I don't have their marriage certificate, but if there is one, no doubt that would be a pack of lies too.'

'This must all be very hard for you Meera.'

'Well, as you can imagine I just want to put it all behind me as soon as possible, and as a first step, I'm now ready to contact my uncle and aunt, if you would be kind enough to give me their details.'

'Of course, Meera. I'll just take these certificates to get them copied and I'll bring Dr Singh's contact details back with me.'

With that Alex left the room and Meera, alone again with her thoughts, fought back the tears that had welled up in her eyes. She quickly dried her eyes and sternly told herself not to waste any more of her tears on 'him'.

Within minutes Alex was back and handed her the certificates, along with a sheet of paper with details of Dr Vijay Singh in Kolkata, India.

'He's quite happy to have video calls Meera, and I'm sure he'd be pleased to hear from you,' Alex assured her, then went on, 'We've already sent him the facial reconstruction picture of your mother, and Sergeant Nugent has just told me that he has confirmed that it is the face of Sunita, his sister, and your mother of course.

'Is there anything else I can help you with Meera?' Alex asked.

'Well, yes actually. Have you any idea when the inquest will be? I want to arrange a cremation of the remains as soon as possible, and ideally, I would like to take them to India, back to my family there, to the place where she called home.'

'We don't have a date yet. In fact, we haven't yet handed the case over to the coroner's office, although that should be done within the next few days. After that it will be in their hands unfortunately. As I think I said before, it's quite possible, in fact it's probable, that the coroner will release the remains for burial before the inquest, but you will be sent the details as soon as we have them. As for the inquest itself, I expect Dr Singh and maybe also Anita Kumar will be asked to give evidence regarding the timing and your mother's reason for coming to England. They may well decide to come over for both the funeral and the inquest, but no doubt you will be able to discuss that with them in person.'

'Yes, of course, I will,' Meera answered, saying, 'Well thank you Inspector, for all your efforts to get to the bottom of all this. I know it won't be possible to definitely allocate blame, but it hardly matters. In my mind I'm sure who was responsible. Else why would he have buried her in that trench and pretended that she never existed?'

Meera offered her hand and Alex shook it warmly.

'Goodbye for now Meera, and we'll make sure you are informed about the inquest as soon as we have the details.'

Driving back to Bristol, Meera went over in her mind what Alex had just told her. Well, that's the final straw, she told herself. No doubt about it now. Her father had murdered her mother. No other word for it.

Chapter 31

After Meera left, Alex called a team meeting to finalise the investigation. Once they were all assembled she began in a business-like tone,

'Ok folks let's see if we can tie this up now. Dr Carter just called in with the certificates she had in her possession. Her birth certificate states that she was born in Bristol and that her mother was Shaheen Carter, both of which we know to be untrue. We must surely assume that Robert and Shaheen Carter faked the certificate. Sally, have we still been unable to find out Shaheen's identity and where she came from?'

'That's right Boss. We have no record of their marriage in this country which would have given us a surname, and we also drew a blank from the Indian authorities. It may be of course, that they never did get married, in which case tracing her would prove very difficult, expensive, and in the end possibly irrelevant?'

'I think you're right Sally. Even if we could find out, no prosecutions would follow as she's already deceased. The same goes for Robert Carter of course and in the absence of any other suspects or even any witnesses to the events at Old St Paul's, the possibility of proving responsibility for the murder is impossible, and I couldn't justify allocating further resources to it.'

'So what now Boss?' Neil asked.

'Well apart from speaking once again to Dr Singh and his sister to put them in the picture, I intend to finalise my report and will recommend to DCI Brimley that we hand it over to the coroner.

'Look, I know this isn't the result we all hoped for. It's always unsettling to be unable to apportion blame and see justice done, but I'm confident we've pursued every avenue open to us, given the circumstances. It will be up to the coroner now to determine the cause of death and whether he feels he can attribute culpability.'

'At least we have been able to tell Dr Carter the truth about her own identity, however painful that is.'

'That's true Ida,' Alex agreed, 'a mixed blessing, I fear. But I guess it's always better to know the truth. No one wants to live a life based on lies. Anyway, thanks, all of you, for your efforts on this case. Once the coroner has studied the report, he may have a few questions, but it will be interesting to see what his final conclusions are.'

By four o'clock Alex was handing over her report to DCI Brimley.

'I'm confident we've taken this as far as we can Sir,' she told him. 'Unfortunately, we were unable to prove responsibility for what has been confirmed as a murder. Not ideal but given that our only suspects are deceased and without finding further witnesses or corroborating evidence, it has proved impossible to do so.'

'Thanks Alex, I'll take a look at it, and hopefully we'll be able to hand it over to the coroner tomorrow.

Later, driving home, Alex was feeling relieved. The job was done, as far as had been possible. She'd spoken briefly to Dr Singh before leaving the office. He was understandably quite distressed at having had confirmation that the remains were his sister's. He confirmed that both he and his sister would be coming over for the inquest and Alex said she would be happy to meet with them to answer any questions they may have. She also told him she'd handed over his details to his niece, Meera, who would probably be contacting him very soon.

'Thank you, DI Scott. My sister and I are very grateful to you for giving Sunita back to us. Thirty-five years is a long time to live without her. We had no idea where she was or what had happened to her. So, thank you, we will always be grateful to you, however painful this has all been.'

'You're very welcome, Dr Singh, I'm only sorry we didn't have better news for you.'

'Well at least we do have our niece, and are looking forward to meeting her soon, of course.'

'Of course Dr Singh, and I will look forward to meeting you both when you come over here. Goodbye for now Doctor.'

'Until then, Inspector.'

Now, as she pulled into her own driveway Alex turned her attention to the personal ordeal that was looming for her. The inquest on her parents' deaths. Before leaving home that morning a letter arrived informing her that it would be held at Bournemouth coroner's court on the following Monday and inviting her to attend. Typically, Dave had insisted that he would go with her, even though she tried to tell him that she'd be fine on her own.

'There's no way I'm going to let you go on your own love,' he'd insisted, 'it's bound to be difficult for you and you shouldn't be driving yourself home afterwards. I'm coming, and that's that.'

Alex, still trying to insist she'd be fine on her own, was secretly grateful. She knew he was right; she may well be in no fit state to concentrate on driving. She was pleased to see Dave's car in the drive. Now the Carter case was over, she was determined to give him and the children more attention than she'd been able to do of late, and of course, apart from the inquest on her mum and dad she had plenty to do. There were the funerals to arrange and get through, and then their house and belongings to sort out. She decided that once the Carter case had finally been sent over to the coroner, hopefully the following day, she would take a week of her annual leave, beginning at the weekend. It was short notice, but she was sure no one would object. She needed to take it on compassionate grounds if nothing else.

'Well, I'm pleased to hear it,' Dave said when she told him she'd decided to take time off, 'about time too. I don't know how you've managed to keep going since the accident.'

'Well, it was a difficult case from several perspectives, and I needed to sort it. I couldn't have walked away from it.'

'I know,' Dave agreed, then took her in his arms, planting a lingering kiss on her lips before adding, 'That's why I love you so much.'

'Ugggh!' exclaimed Johnny, who'd been sitting at the table finishing his supper, 'Get a room, you two!'

Alex and Dave smiled, and Aby said,

'What does that mean?

'You're too young, little sister,' Johnny replied, grinning, then ducked as Aby made a swipe at his head.

Two o'clock the following day found Meera staring at her laptop anxiously listening to the dialling tone of WhatsApp. Any moment now she would meet perfect strangers who were going to be part of her life from now on. DI Scott had handed her the details of her uncle Dr Vijay Singh and later, back at her flat, she had spent an hour or so researching him on the Internet. She was pleasantly surprised to find many references to him and his work as a psychiatrist. Following up some of the links, she read several articles he had written. It was clear that he was well respected among his peers.

She emailed him later that evening to arrange a WhatsApp call. He had obviously been very happy to hear from her and said he would be delighted to speak to her the following day at around two o'clock, UK time, after he'd finished work for the day, and he hoped that Anita would be joining him.

So, this was it, she thought, the beginning of her new life. Suddenly there they were in front of her. Her aunt and uncle, the sister and brother of her mother. She had been apprehensive, wondering how she'd feel, seeing them. They were strangers after all. She needn't have worried. A feeling she could only describe as joyful recognition bubbled up inside her as they both smiled at her. For the moment she was speechless, trying to control her emotions.

'Meera, how wonderful to see you at last,' her uncle said, the sincerity in his voice unmistakeable.

Meera uncharacteristically struggled with her words.

'Err... 'I'm sorry, I don't know how to address you,' she mumbled.

'Well Meera,' he said confidently, 'As it appears I am your uncle, I would be honoured if you would address me in that way.'

'Of course, Uncle, it's wonderful to meet you, even in such sad circumstances.'

'I only wish we could have met years ago Meera, but we didn't know where you were.'

Sitting beside her uncle was a woman who she judged to be about sixty years old. The likeness to her mother's picture told Meera that this was indeed her aunt. She now spoke up,

'Meera, I'm your aunt Anita. I was your dear mother's older sister.'

'Aunt,' Meera replied, 'it's wonderful to meet you also.'

'All this must have come as a terrible shock to you Meera. I can't imagine how you're coping with it all to be honest,' Anita went on empathetically.

'I'm guessing the police will have put you in the picture about 'him' then?'

'They did Meera,' her uncle confirmed.

'I see, and of course you're right, it has been a dreadful shock, but I'm trying to look forward now. My past seems like just one big lie so I feel I need to draw a line under it.'

'That's understandable Meera,' her uncle interjected, 'and you can be sure that your aunt and I will do whatever we can to help you.'

'Well, Di Scott said that you both intend to come over for the inquest. Is that right?'

'Most definitely,' he agreed.

'Well, it appears that the remains may be released before the inquest, and I want to arrange to have them cremated. It is my dearest wish now to take my mother's ashes back to India, to where she grew up and where she called home.'

'That is a truly wonderful idea Meera. We would certainly wish to be present at the funeral as well as the inquest, and we'll be only too happy to accompany you back here if it can be arranged in time.'

'One thing I wanted to ask you Uncle, was my mother of the Hindu faith.'

'Yes, all our family practice that religion.'

'I see, well, in that case, I will want to reflect that in the funeral service. Perhaps you could advise me about that?'

'Of course Meera, I will be happy to do that.'

'Thank you, Uncle. It will be lovely to meet you both in person. I have so many questions to ask you both about my mother and of course, I want to learn as much as I can about my roots.'

'It will be our pleasure to answer all of your questions Meera,' Anita told her.

A thought suddenly struck Meera,

'Are my grandparents still alive, Aunt?'

'Sadly not, Meera. They both passed away some years ago, but you do have cousins and other relatives.'

'I look forward to hearing all about them,' Meera replied, then went on, 'I will let you know about the funeral arrangements and the inquest details as soon as I have them.'

'Thank you, Meera. We are both looking forward to meeting you properly and hopefully to spend some time with you. We all have a lot of catching up to do.'

Meera smiled comfortably, there was something so kind and familiar about these people and already she felt herself relax in their presence, even over a WhatsApp video call.

'We certainly have uncle, and I'll have a long list of questions when we finally meet, you can be sure.'

'Well, thank you for ringing Meera, and hopefully it won't be long before we're there with you.'

'Hopefully not uncle,' she agreed, adding, 'Goodbye until then.'

After the call ended, Meera sat for some moments wondering at how easy it had been to talk to these perfect strangers; as though she had known them all her life. I suppose it's all in the genes, she mused.

Needing to share her feelings with someone, she called Pete who she knew was always ready to listen.

'Meera!' he exclaimed, 'Great to hear from you. How're things?'

'Hi Pete, sorry to bother you but I just had to tell someone.'

'Tell me what? Has something happened?'

'No, not really, but I've just been on a WhatsApp video link to my uncle and aunt in India!'

'Oh that's great Meera. How did it go?'

'It was amazing Pete. I felt as though I've known them all my life! It's the first positive thing that's happened to me for weeks. I'm so excited that they're hopefully coming over for the funeral, so I'll get to meet them in person. Isn't that wonderful?'

'Of course it is. I'm guessing they'll be important people in your life going forward, even though they'll be thousands of miles away.'

'I've been thinking though Pete. I intend to have my mother's remains cremated and then to take them back to India. It seems the least I can do for her now, to take her back home. That's where her roots are of course, and mine too now.'

Pete's stomach churned as he anticipated what was coming next, but he had to know and said quietly,

'I see Meera. But you won't be staying there, will you?'

'I don't know, it's too early for me to say Pete. I only know that I must put my old life behind me, based as it was on a pack of lies. I must start to build myself a new life now, based on the person I should have been.'

'But you can do that here, surely?'

'I don't know yet. I can only take things one step at a time. First of all, there's the funeral then the inquest, after which I'll take the ashes to India. As to what comes next, I just don't know.'

After chatting for a few minutes about the dig and the fact that they would all finally be off site by the weekend, once again he asked if he could see her in Bristol. She agreed to give him a ring when he was back but hadn't seemed particularly keen.

Pete could see the future he'd been hoping would include Meera slipping away from him. He realised it was possible she may include him in her 'old life' and decide to leave him behind along with her career in archaeology. After he'd put the phone down, he was full of foreboding that he was about to lose the only woman he'd ever truly loved, and before he'd even had the chance to tell her how much. He told himself that he wasn't ready to give up so easily and determined to tell her how he felt at the first opportunity. If he didn't, he realised, he would never forgive himself.

Chapter 32

Alex had attended several inquests in the past, including a couple at this Coroner's Court. This was very different. She was here as a relative of the deceased. As an 'interested person' she was able to see any evidence in advance of the inquest and had been sent a copy by the police. The report concluded that it had been just a terrible accident. Of course, there may have been contributing factors, and she was hoping to find more out about them today.

As only one date had been set for the hearing, it appeared that the coroner would be dealing with the deaths of both her mum and dad concurrently as they had died together in the same incident. She realised that as her father had been driving, the coroner would need to rule out any kind of medical event which could have caused him to make a fatal error. Failing that, the coroner would establish the cause of the accident, set out the sequence of events leading up to it and establish whether there were any factors such as poor road conditions, bad lighting, or confusing road signs which ought to be addressed in order to avoid any further accidents.

All this was going through her mind as she sat outside the courtroom waiting for Dave to appear after parking the car. Sitting opposite her was a man in his early thirties. From his appearance and demeanour, she wondered if he was the driver of the goods vehicle her father's car had collided with. This gave her an uneasy feeling. Could this man be the last person to see her parents alive? Did he see the look of horror as they realised what was going to happen within the next seconds? From what she had already been told, her father had pulled out in front of a heavy goods vehicle travelling at some speed.

'You alright love?' Dave asked as he sat down beside her and took her hand.

'I'm OK Dave. I just wish it was over.'

'I know,' he replied, squeezing her hand tightly, glancing at his watch on his other wrist. 'Shouldn't be long now.'

A clerk announced the case was about to start and invited interested parties to enter. Alex knew the layout of the courtroom and made her way to the seating to the right of the front desk where the coroner would be sitting. The young man she had noticed earlier sat down in a chair at the end of the row. Two policemen sat together in the row in front of them. One of them was in uniform and was obviously a constable. The other was dressed in plain clothes and Alex realised he was the Senior Investigating Officer.

'All rise!' the clerk declared as the coroner entered the room and took up his position on the dais.

The coroner began by offering his condolences to the relatives of the deceased, emphasising the desperately sad nature of the events which led to the tragic deaths of an elderly couple.

'For anyone unfamiliar with the purpose of an inquest,' the coroner continued, 'let me briefly explain. I am here to confirm the identity of the deceased person. In this case, this is a joint inquest into the deaths of two people who died simultaneously. By considering all the evidence put before me I will confirm the place, time, and circumstances of their deaths. It is also my role to establish exactly how the person or persons died. I am not here to determine blame or criminal liability.'

After pausing for a moment, the coroner removed the half spectacles perched on his nose, surveyed the room, then continued,

'Very well, let us begin.'

Looking directly at the plain-clothes officer sitting in front of Alex, he went on,

'Inspector Grimwald, I believe you are the Senior Investigating Officer in this case?'

'I am, sir,' the Inspector acknowledged.

'Then please come forward.'

Inspector Grimwald took the witness stand and placed his hand on the bible presented to him by the clerk, held his right hand up, then proclaimed the oath,

'I swear to tell the truth, the whole truth and nothing but the truth, so help me God.'

Dave squeezed Alex's hand, and she acknowledged his gesture by giving a slight nod of her head.

The next thirty minutes or so, were the most difficult Alex had ever experienced. To hear her parents' names read out in court, and their final moments on this earth discussed in such a detached way was almost too much to bear. She managed to control her emotions by concentrating hard on what Inspector Grimwald was saying, not wishing to miss any detail.

As she already knew from the documents they had sent her, her father had unexpectedly pulled out at a crossroads, intending to turn right. The junction was marked as a crossroad with a 'no right turn' sign.

At this point, the coroner interjected,

'Inspector, did you investigate whether Mr Trenton would have been familiar with this road prior to the incident?'

'We did sir, and as far as we could determine, this area may not have been one he was familiar with. It was several miles from his home, and he had been driving his wife back from a hospital appointment along a route he may not normally have taken.'

'Why is that?

'Because, sir, there had been congestion along his normal route from the hospital to his home.'

Alex almost gasped out loud at this. So, it appeared she had lost her parents because of a traffic jam! Anger welled up inside her. To think that she'd lost her mum and dad because of something as mundane as a traffic jam! She knew that wasn't the whole story, but it was still one of those unbearable 'what ifs' she'd seen others trying to come to terms with after the sudden loss of a loved one.

'I see,' the judge acknowledged, 'thank you. Carry on Inspector.'

Inspector Grimwald went on to explain that Mr Trenton had pulled out of the junction, turning right, unfortunately into the path of an articulated vehicle that had been approaching the junction from that direction. The collision was almost instantaneous, and the impact had forced the car across the road and into a concrete pillar. He explained that the collision with the goods vehicle had impacted the driver's side and that violent contact with the concrete pillar on the other side of the road had crushed the passenger's side. In this way, firstly the driver, and then the passenger had sustained catastrophic internal injuries.

Alex felt sick. The realisation that for a split second her mother would have understood what was happening, before herself facing oblivion, was more than Alex could stand, and she quickly got up and quietly left the courtroom. Dave followed her out only to see her heading for the ladies' cloakroom.

He waited outside the door for her to reappear. It was a good fifteen minutes later that she did so, looking decidedly unwell, her eyes red-rimmed and her face pale.

'I'm sorry,' she immediately said to Dave, 'I didn't expect that.'

'I know you didn't. Neither did I to be honest. Are you up to going back in, or do you just want to leave the legals to it?'

'I have to see this through Dave,' she replied firmly.

With that, they slid back into the courtroom, this time sitting at the back so as not to attract attention.

The young man was visibly shaken as he answered the coroner's questions regarding the accident. He did turn out to be the driver of the goods vehicle and the coroner asked him to describe in his own words what had happened. Listening to his second-by-second account was excruciating for Alex.

When the young man had finished his testimony, the coroner called the pathologist who had carried out the postmortems. She was a smart looking woman about forty years old.'

After she had answered several questions put by the coroner, he went on,

'In your opinion then, Doctor Craddock, in both cases, the deceased would have died instantly. Is that correct?'

'Up to a point sir. Of course, given that the driver was first to be impacted and would have died instantly, the impact on Mrs Trenton, who was sitting in the passenger seat, followed a couple of seconds later after the car had been shunted across the road, so although she was then killed instantly, she would have died a few seconds after her husband.'

Once again Alex was forced to contemplate the horror of her mother's last few seconds of consciousness and her stomach churned once again. She didn't really hear what was said for the next few minutes. Then the pathologist had finished her evidence, and the coroner asked whether anyone had any questions.

The coroner looked directly at Alex, who, with a slight shake of her head indicated that she had no questions. She had heard enough and just wanted to get out of the courtroom. She knew the verdict could only be 'accidental death' on both counts, and so it turned out to be. However, there was still that knot of anger in her stomach, at the utter waste of it, certainly, but also at her father for taking her mother away from her by making such a stupid mistake as to turn the wrong way into oncoming traffic.

As they headed home along the A338, Alex was uncharacteristically silent, but Dave could sense the anger still raging within her. He had hoped that the inquest might have given her some closure. He knew she was in some way blaming Ted for the loss of her mother, as he had been driving, and the accident was plainly the result of him turning the wrong way at the junction. It seemed that if anything, what she'd heard at the inquest had made her even more angry.

'Want to talk about it?' he queried softly.

'Not much point really, what's done is done. Talking won't bring them back.'

'I know, but it might help you to get whatever is making you angry off your chest.'

'I don't see how. because the one person I need to talk to about it isn't here anymore.'

'Your dad?'

'Of course,' Alex answered impatiently.

'Maybe you could talk to someone else about it?' Dave suggested.

'Counselling, you mean? Again, I don't see what good that would do.'

'Well, I know it's something you often advise victims of crimes to do, so you must believe it can work.'

'That's true. Oh, I don't know, maybe you're right. I'll give it some thought anyway,' Alex replied but without much conviction.

Chapter 33

On the other hand, there was no doubt at all in Meera's mind who had been responsible for her mother's death and her own betrayal. It was so obvious and so final that she had no difficulty cutting off all thoughts, and even memories, of him. She was now resolutely looking forward to her new life and joining what she now regarded as her real family in Kolkata.

Her uncle had sent her details about their expected arrival, and she was determined to collect them from the airport. They were flying from Kolkata to Dubai where they were to pick up a flight to London Gatwick, arriving at around six thirty in the evening.

She was waiting nervously in the Arrivals Hall. All around there was a buzz of excitement as friends and relatives bustled to get a good view of the steady stream of passengers who had begun to appear. Having finally reached their destination at last after a twelve-hour journey, they were obviously looking rather travel-weary, until, that is, their eyes rested on a familiar group of faces, at which point they broke into a broad grin as they were swallowed up in a sea of embraces and joyous sounds. There were people travelling alone with no one to greet them. Probably business travellers, Meera mused. Then there were the young people carrying rucksacks looking happy and tanned, and dressed only in shorts and tee shirts, totally unsuitable for the English climate. No doubt, Meera conjectured, returning from travelling round Asia during their gap year. She felt quite envious of them. That was something she'd always wanted to do but her father had refused to finance a gap year, eager for her to follow in his footsteps and immediately immerse herself in an archaeology degree. Well, she thought, thanks to him she would not only be taking a gap year, but hopefully, many gap years. Quite ironic really.

She had printed off pictures of her aunt and uncle, but was still rather worried that she wouldn't recognise them. The steady stream of passengers had now turned into a flood, and she peered anxiously among the faces. She realised she had no idea whether they were tall or short, slim, or stocky. She had only ever seen their faces!

She needn't have worried because the face of her uncle Vijay suddenly appeared above the throng. He was smiling broadly now and holding up a hand in greeting. She smiled back and waved happily while manoeuvring herself to the front of the crush. Then she saw her aunt, and the family resemblance was unmistakeable.

Not sure how to greet these two strangers who would become so important to her future, in the end she concluded there was no point holding back and she quickly stepped forward with arms outstretched. Her aunt enveloped her in a fierce embrace saying,

'At last! Meera, it's wonderful to be here with you, finally.'

After luxuriating in the warmth of her aunt's greeting, Meera turned to her uncle. He was smiling warmly and holding out his arms and she willingly allowed herself to be scooped up in another warm hug.

'Meera. You don't know how much it means to us to find you. Your dear mother would be so happy to see us together like this.'

Meera was a little embarrassed to feel tears trickling down her cheeks and for a moment was quite unable to speak.

Finally, she managed,

'It's amazing to have you both here. Thank you so much for coming all this way.'

'We wouldn't have missed it Meera,' Vijay replied.

Realising just how emotional Meera must be feeling, Vijay went on to say,

'Come, let us get out of here. Did you drive?'

Meera nodded,

'I'm parked in the airport carpark. It's quite a long walk.'

'No problem, let's go,' he replied, and they set off down the concourse, Anita linking Meera's arm affectionately and Vijay following behind dragging their suitcases.

During the long drive back to Bristol, they chatted easily as though they had known each other for years. Meera was eager to find out everything they could tell her about Sunita. What was she like? What sort of things did she enjoy doing? Was she a happy person? Did she have a good sense of humour?

Question after question fell from Meera's lips and Vijay and Anita patiently answered each one fully. Meera was beginning to get a sense of the kind of person her mother had been. She recognized much of herself in the descriptions.

Vijay and Anita sensitively avoided any conversation about Carter, realising that Meera would be finding even thinking about him difficult, let alone talking about him. They realised that in the course of their visit, particularly during the inquest, they would find out what the police had discovered about the circumstances of Sunita's death.

The main thing now, they felt, was to get to know their niece and to offer her all the support they could, over the next difficult weeks.

Meera wanted to know about Kolkata, and their homes there, and Anita described in great detail, the house where she and her husband lived, and suggested that if she was to return with them, she would be very welcome to stay with them for as long as she wished.

Vijay talked about his work. He said he was beginning to wind down his psychiatry practice to spend more time with his wife, his children, and grandchildren, of which he had four. Apparently, he and his wife lived just a mile or so from Anita, and both families were obviously very close.

This all sounded wonderful to Meera, who had grown up without any extended family. No grandparents, aunts, uncles, or cousins. She hadn't realised until now just how much she had missed all that.

After a stop at the services on the M4, where they grabbed a coffee and something to eat, they were soon back on the road. Vijay and Anita would like to have asked Meera about her life but realised that was best avoided for now. Any conversation about her childhood or her career would inevitably involve her talking about Carter, and she would be trying to avoid that at all costs. Vijay understood that she would, in time, be able to talk about it all, but the revelations about her father and mother were still too raw to be discussed with anyone, and particularly with them.

It was late when they arrived at the Premier Inn. Vijay insisted that as it was so late, it would be best if Meera just dropped them off and that they would ring her in the morning to arrange to meet up, probably to have lunch, if she was free. Meera gladly agreed,

'That would be lovely uncle, I'll give you a ring around ten if that's ok?'

'That will be perfect Meera'

With that they all got out of the car and Vijay retrieved their cases from the boot. They wished each other goodnight with more hugs, and Meera left with a warm feeling of belonging. Her future life was beginning to look more inviting she mused, as she drove back to her apartment.

When she arrived, she was so excited about everything they had told her, that she just had to tell someone.

'Meera!' he said, 'Great to hear from you. What news?

'Oh Pete, I just had to tell someone! I just picked my uncle and aunt up from Gatwick and drove them back here. We never stopped talking the whole way. It was as though I'd known them all my life, and they told me so much about my mother. It was wonderful!'

As he listened to her, he could hear excitement bubbling up with every word she spoke, once again Pete could sense that events would soon be taking her away from him.

'I'm so pleased for you Meera,' he managed, then he decided he would have to tell her how he felt, before matters progressed too far. He went on,

'Look, Meera, I can't go on like this.'

'What do you mean Pete?'

'Well, you know how I've felt about you right from the start, don't you? I love you Meera, and I need to know how you really feel about me.'

'Oh Pete, you know how much you've meant to me over these past weeks, but I'm still all over the place right now and it's difficult to know how I feel.'

His heart sank. If she really loved me, he thought, she wouldn't have any doubts. He felt exposed. He shouldn't have said anything. Now he'd lose her friendship as well. But maybe if they could meet and talk, properly, just maybe she could clarify how she felt. He knew he was probably clutching at straws, but suddenly he felt he had to try.

'Please Meera, can we meet and talk properly?'

'Honestly Pete, I think that may just make things worse at the moment, until I'm sure how I feel. Can you please be patient with me. Let me get this funeral and the inquest out of the way, and then perhaps I'll be able to think more clearly.'

He did understand how traumatic all this had been for her, and he realised that he had no choice but to agree.

'Ok Meera, I do understand. Ring me when you've decided what to do.'

Abruptly, he ended the call giving Meera no time to reply and leaving her feeling strangely bereft. She hadn't even had time to tell him all the things she'd discovered about her mother.

As planned, Meera met Vijay and Anita the next day at a cosy bistro near to the Premier Inn. Meera realised that during the journey from the airport, the conversation had been all about life in India and her plans to return there with them. It was understandable that no one wanted to talk about her present life, given that 'he' had always played an intimate role in it. However, she was desperate to ask them about what had happened to her mother. Did they know where she had gone when she left the family home? Where had she herself been born? Did they know anything at all about what happened to her after she'd arrived in England?

After they had eaten and were enjoying a coffee, Meera launched into these questions that were bothering her greatly, given that she knew so little about the last months and weeks of her mother's life. As it turned out, sadly neither did they. As Vijay had already told her, once she'd left the family home, he had no knowledge of where she'd gone, or how she'd survived financially. Then a month or so after Meera was born, she had contacted him to ask him to help her. Although this meant him going against his parents' wishes, he said he could not have refused her.

'I did, of course, ask who your father was Meera, but she refused to tell me. She would only say that he was an Englishman with whom she had had a brief liaison but that he had returned to England shortly afterwards and knew nothing about the baby. She was sure though that once he did know, he would help her to look after his child.'

'She must have been desperate,' Meera said sadly.

'She was. And so, I had to help her. I found her enough money to book a return flight to England, and to survive for a while until she had located your father. Sadly, when I said goodbye to her the day I handed over the money, it was the last time I saw or even heard from her.'

'Didn't you try to find out what had happened to her, uncle?'

'It was difficult because my parents were still alive and determined that no one should have anything to do with her. They were very traditional and felt she had brought shame on the family. I know that's difficult to understand Meera, but that's the way it was for that generation.'

'Yes, I do understand of course, but it still seems very harsh, to be banished from the family for one mistake.'

Then Anita spoke up,

'Of course, you know that once my parents had both passed away, we decided to take the DNA test and to place it on the International Database in the hope that one day she might come looking for us.'

'And thank goodness we did Meera,' Vijay added.

'Well, I'm very grateful that you did uncle. At least I now have a family and a future.'

'Indeed you have,' Vijay concluded with a warm smile.

Meera smiled broadly, something she hadn't been doing much of lately.

'About the funeral Uncle. I want to keep it very simple. I am assuming that once we get the ashes back to Kolkata, you will want to arrange a Hindu ceremony for her?'

'Yes of course, if you are in agreement.'

'Certainly. I'm sure that's what she would have wanted. But I was wondering if you would say a couple of prayers at the crematorium?'

'I would be happy to do so Meera, thank you for asking me.'

'Are you aware,' Anita said quietly, 'that at Hindu funerals, the mourners wear white, not black?'

'I wasn't Aunt,' Meera replied, 'but thank you for telling me. I have so much to learn!'

Chapter 34

Once the funeral arrangements were finalised, Meera rang Alex to invite her to come along if possible, knowing how hard she had worked to discover how her mother had died. As it happened, it was to be on the same day as Ted and Dorothy's funeral in Tidmouth. Not quite sure why she decided to tell Meera about her mum and dad, Alex explained how they had both died in a car accident and were to be laid to rest together. She supposed she told her because she felt they had both been travelling the same road; both were angry at their fathers, although her rage at Ted was beginning to subside. It was an accident, after all. Meera's anger on the other hand, Alex was sure, would never go away, combined as it must be with a feeling of utter betrayal.

'I'm so sorry to hear that Inspector,' Meera replied, her voice full of concern, 'It must have been so difficult for you, grieving your parents while dealing with all this.'

'Part of the job, I'm afraid, separating our lives into compartments. If we didn't, we would never cope,' Alex asserted.

She went on to express her admiration for Meera and the way she'd conducted herself through this undoubtedly very difficult time, and they enjoyed a moment of empathy that comforted them both.

'I expect you're quite nervous about the inquest,' Alex said quietly.

'Well, I'm sure that, because of you Inspector, there won't be any more nasty surprises. I am grateful that you've kept me in the picture even though hearing the truth has been difficult at times. At least it's given me the chance to process it all. So, I thank you for that.'

'You're very welcome. I realised from the start your life may well be turned upside down and that you would need to be given the truth.'

Five days later Alex, Dave and the children walked behind the two coffins into the crematorium in Tidmouth. There were a few of Ted and Dorothy's friends, Ted's brother and his wife and a cousin of Dorothy's. Alex walked with her arm around Aby's shoulder to comfort her as she began to cry silently. Behind them Dave and Johnny walked in silence, heads bowed.

The service, as usual in a crematorium was short, but Alex had included music that had meant something to her parents. The strains of 'Morning has Broken' were playing quietly as the matching coffins were carried in. Dave gave the eulogy and the humanist celebrant said a few words about Ted and Dorothy and their lives together. Johnny bravely read out the Rudyard Kipling poem 'Gunga Din' that had been a particular favourite of his grandad.

It was very emotional for them all, of course, particularly as the curtains closed on the coffins, but as they all left the crematorium to Edward Elgar's 'Nimrod', Alex felt it had been a fitting tribute to them both. After a lunch at the nearby 'Kings Arms' one by one the mourners left until finally Alex, Dave, Johnny, and Aby lingered to reminisce about Ted and Dorothy and the times they had all shared. Finally, it was time to leave and head back home, to the rest of their lives, leaving Ted and Dorothy as memories to be fondly brought out and dusted from time to time.

Meanwhile, at the crematorium in Somerset, Sunita's funeral was very different. Meera hadn't a clue what kind of music to use, or what to say about her mother, as she had never met her. She decided to keep it simple, with just a piece of pastoral orchestral music playing quietly as they entered the building. The only family mourners were Meera, Vijay and Anita, and Sally Nugent came along to represent the police.

She had wondered whether to invite Pete, but given her confusion over how she felt about him, she decided against it. She was anxious not to lead him on when she was so unsure about her own feelings towards him. She hadn't seen him since she'd met him at the Crooked Gate on that fateful day when she had learnt the truth about the identity of the body in the grave. Thoughts of him had been intruding often over the subsequent weeks, and he had rung a couple of times, but she had resisted seeing him. It would have been comforting though, to have had him here now, she thought to herself as they entered the crematorium.

The funeral director had been able to advise her on the form of the service itself, as they had conducted many Hindu funerals in the past. Anita, Vijay, and Meera all wore white and stood around the coffin while Vijay read a couple of Hindu prayers, and a recited a mantra.

When it was over Meera shook hands with Sally, thanking her for coming and for all the police had done.

'I am pleased that I was able to be here, as would DI Scott if she hadn't had to go to Tidmouth. I'm so glad we were at least able to connect you to your Indian family Meera.'

'Yes, thanks to you I'm able to look forward to building a new life. I intend to take my mother's ashes back to India soon, and will probably stay there a while, getting to know the country and my extended family.'

Afterwards Meera drove to a small hotel where she and her aunt and uncle enjoyed a quiet meal together. They all knew that the ordeal of the inquest was still to come in five days' time and each in their own way was nervous about what they might hear and how they would react. Since the revelation by DI Scott about the role her father had probably played in Sunita's death, Meera had been trying as much as possible to put him out of her head. Now she would have to sit through several hours of evidence. There would be no escape from it. How would she cope? She had no idea.

Vijay and Anita, while determined to listen to every bit of evidence put forward by the police, like Meera, they had no doubt who had been responsible for their sister's death. Except, maybe, their own parents who, instead of supporting their daughter, had cast her out. And Vijay was reflecting on his own part in all this. When Sunita had come to him for help, he could have done much more for her. He could have supported her himself rather than writing a cheque and watching her walk away to a foreign country and her eventual death. Anita didn't feel much better about it. She could have stood up to her parents when they told Sunita to leave, but instead, she did and said nothing. Shamefully now she had to admit, if only to herself, that as Sunita, who she had long thought was her parents' favourite, would be leaving the family, she believed she would be able to take her place in the affections of her mother and father. She had done nothing to help her sister.

They all knew that they would have to face these uncomfortable truths as the inquest unfolded.

Chapter 35

After the funeral Meera turned her attention to preparing for her journey to India after the inquest. She had applied for the necessary permission from the Indian authorities to transport the ashes. She would need a residency permit eventually, but for the moment was ostensibly just a visitor. She had decided to spend a month or so in Kolkata before returning briefly to terminate the tenancy on her apartment and deal with her belongings. The property had been let fully furnished, so the furniture, fixtures and fittings would be staying. Once she was sure she wouldn't be returning to England permanently, she would pack and ship her personal belongings to India.

Vijay and Anita were keen to visit the site where their sister had been buried, but Meera declined to go with them. Understanding her reluctance, they contacted the police to arrange a visit, unsure whether the site was still closed for public access. They were put through to Alex, who answered,

'DI Scott here. How can I help.'

'Ah DI Scott, it's Vijay Singh here.'

'Dr Singh! Good to hear from you. Sergeant Nugent told me that you were at the funeral. I was sorry that I couldn't attend.'

'Yes, DI Scott, and could I express our condolences to you about the death of your parents.'

'Thank you Dr Singh. Yes, it has been a distressing time for all of us, hasn't it? '

After a pause, Alex went on,

'What can I do for you today Dr Singh. Do you have any questions?'

'Not right now, thank you. In fact, we were wondering if it would be in order for us to visit the burial site? We will be going home soon after the inquest, but we do have a few days before then and would dearly like to visit the place where our dear sister had been lying for all those years. Understandably Dr Carter doesn't want to see the place again as it was the site of such a traumatic experience for her.'

'Of course, I understand perfectly Dr Singh. Look, I would be more than happy to meet you and your sister at the site. Do you have transport?

'We do, I've hired a car during our stay here.'

'I could be there early tomorrow morning, if that's convenient,' Alex offered.

Vijay said that would be perfect. He made a note of the address and postcode of Old St Paul's church and said they would be there for nine-thirty the following morning.

After he'd ended the call, Vijay rang Meera to explain what they were doing and to ask if she was sure that she didn't want to return to the site with them.

'Thanks for asking Uncle, but after what I experienced in that place, wild horses wouldn't drag me back there. Not now at any rate. Maybe in years to come, if the opportunity arose, I may well go there again, but right now, it's more than I could bear.'

'I understand Meera, but as you will appreciate it's important for us to see where she has been all these years. DI Scott is meeting us there to point out the exact place.'

'Of course, I do understand why you and Aunt Anita want to visit the site. It will also help you at the inquest, to visualise the layout and the position of the burial site.'

It had been a hectic time for all of them, and Meera was relieved when the day of the inquest finally arrived. She was standing outside the Coroner's Court with Vijay and Anita when Alex and Sally arrived, looking sombre, as the occasion demanded. They stepped up to the little group and shook hands with them one by one.

Meera smiled at Hilary Black who had also just arrived along with Dr Felicity Butcher, the osteo-archaeologist, and a man she didn't recognise but who turned out to be the geneticist. Meera checked her watch. It was nearly ten. The inquest was due to begin soon. As she looked up, she was shocked to see Pete walking through the swing doors at the entrance to the building.

It just had not occurred to her that he would be summoned to attend. Of course, now she realised, it had been inevitable. He had been the first to discover the body. Of course, the coroner would want to hear what he had to say.

With arranging the funeral and preparations for leaving the country she'd had so much to deal with that since their last conversation, she had tried, but not completely succeeded, to put him out of her mind. Without hesitation, as soon as he saw Meera standing there, he walked quickly across to her,

The look on his face was unmistakeable. He had eyes for no one else and couldn't hide his joy at seeing her again.

'Meera, how are you?' he said softly.

The sound of his caring voice, and the look of love in his eyes, affected Meera more deeply than she could have expected. She had felt 'over him'. Now the old spark she had first felt all those weeks ago had returned in an instant and with a vengeance.

'Pete! It's good to see you,' she replied, and in that moment oblivious to everything and everyone around them, they hugged each other warmly. After a few seconds, somewhat embarrassed now, they quickly stepped back and Meera hurriedly introduced him to Vijay and Anita, who had both been watching them with knowing expressions on their faces.

At that moment, the clerk of the court opened the door and summoned them to enter. Meera flashed Pete one of those smiles that always set his heart racing, then turned and walked into the courtroom.

The next two hours proved to be every bit as difficult as Meera had envisaged. Even though she was already in possession of the main facts, to listen to them spelled out in detail forced her to confront once more the horror of what had happened to her mother. One by one the witnesses were called.

The coroner asked Alex to present the police's case, detailing what evidence they had discovered. He then asked her to outline their conclusion, that the most likely sequence of events was that Sunita Singh had contacted Robert Carter and his wife on arrival in England, and that either by design or accident, she had perished at their hands and her body disposed in an open trench on the archaeological site his team had been excavating.

The various witnesses included Hilary Black, Felicity Butcher, and Mr Ford, who gave their corroborating evidence for the police's statement. Leonard Larkin was called to confirm the details about the trench where the body had been buried, and Pete was called to describe how it had been discovered. Vijay was asked to read out his statement and had not found it easy.

Meera listened to it all intently, wincing at each mention of her father. She had been determinedly avoiding any thoughts of him, but now she had no choice but to hear his name repeated over, and over again. Her mother had been ten years younger than she was now when she died, just twenty-five, and the thought of her young life being snuffed out so brutally was almost more than she could bear. However, Meera knew she must bear it for it her sake. Horrific as it was, this would be the moment she would be nearest to understanding and having a connection to her mother. She could never speak to her or even see her, but she could gain some understanding of what kind of a person she was.

The coroner was summing up now. About Sunita he was saying,

'She had been prepared to leave everyone and everything she knew to try to find the one person she believed would help her to give her daughter a future. Instead of helping her, it is my belief that he or they, killed her and kept Meera for their own. Could that have been,' he speculated, 'one reason why they killed Sunita so that they could keep the child?'

Meera reeled at this. They never had any other children, so it was possible, she now realised, with new horror welling up inside her. Could her mother have been sacrificed to their desire for a child, for her?

Pete, who was sitting beside her, could feel that she was trembling now. It was what he had suspected all along; that the Carters, having maybe even accidentally killed Sunita may have disposed of her body not only to save their own necks but also in order to steal her child. Unable to resist, he now reached out to her. She clung to his hand as though her life depended on it.

Speaking to her aunt and uncle over the last week about Sunita's faith, she knew her mother had been a devout Hindu, and that one of the main tenets of that religion is a belief in life after death and re-incarnation. She thought about the feelings and nightmares she'd had and was now certain that it was her mother who had been guiding her to Old St Paul's. She hoped that once they had taken her home Sunita would be able to be at peace at last.

Finally, it was over. The coroner gave his verdict, 'Unlawful Killing'. In his opinion Sunita had died as a result of being strangled, and although there was insufficient evidence to prove it beyond all doubt, the most likely perpetrators were Robert Carter and/or Shaheen Carter, and her body concealed by them in an un-marked grave.

The coroner thanked them for coming and then left the court..

Everyone hovered around outside the building for a few moments. Meera looked relieved that it was all over. Pete was standing in front of her, just about to say something when he noticed Alex coming up behind her, obviously wanting to speak to her. He said quietly,

'Meera, I think DI Scott wants a word.'

With that she turned quickly to face Alex.

'Inspector, thank goodness that's over, but I want to thank you again for getting to the truth about what happened to my mother.'

'Well, not quite, but we've done our best, in the circumstances,' Alex replied, then went on to ask what Meera would do now.

Meera told her that she had resigned from the University and was definitely not continuing her archaeological career. She would be returning Sunita's ashes to India, intending to try to build a new life for herself there with her aunt and uncle and her extended family.

Pete looked crestfallen as she spoke and his reaction did not go unnoticed by Vijay and Anita, who once again exchanged knowing glances.

'Inspector, I want to say again, how sorry I was to hear about your parents.'

'Thank you Meera, I guess it's been a dreadful time for both of us. I do hope you can find some peace in India, with your newly discovered family,' Alex continued, smiling at Vijay and Anita. 'Anyway, I just wanted to wish you all the best.'

Alex held out her hand and Meera shook it warmly. The handshake turned into a hug as the two women showed they understood what each other had been through over the past weeks.

After all the others had gone, Vijay and Anita said they had to go back to their hotel, leaving Meera and Pete to spend time alone together, which they clearly needed to do.

Chapter 36

Now Meera and Pete were unable to resist any longer the emotional pull that had been there virtually from the first moment they had met. Circumstances had conspired to keep them apart, not least the personal turmoil Meera had been going through.

Now though, the barriers that had been there had melted away. Meera was no longer Pete's professional superior. The inquest had given her some closure. She had mentally let go of her old life, or thought she had, until Pete had walked through the swing doors that morning.

As soon as she had heard his voice gently asking her how she was, the old thrill had returned and as she had fallen into his arms, she had felt complete. As he held her hand, throughout the inquest, she felt supported and loved. It felt good to have him by her side.

No words were needed as they made their way back to Ashley Grove. Once inside, he took her in his arms, whispering the words he had been longing to say.

'I love you Meera,'

Feeling no resistance, he kissed her gently on her lips and she responded eagerly. She led him into her bedroom and there all the pent-up emotion poured out of them in an ecstasy of passion.

Afterwards, they lay in each other's arms utterly and wonderfully content.

Raising herself up on one elbow, she turned to look down into his face and finally said the words he'd been dreaming he would one day hear from her lips,

'I love you Pete Shore. I think I always have.'

She had been due to leave for India ten days later. Pete knew she would have to go. Her mission to return her mother's ashes would have to come first, but he was hoping desperately that she would change her mind about making a new life in India. Surely now, she would want to be here with him, in England.

For the first few days, it seemed that neither of them had wanted to burst their happiness bubble by mentioning it, but eventually with just four days to go before her departure, Pete could stand it no longer, and still dreading hearing her reply, forced himself to ask,

'I'm sorry Meera, but I have to know. Will you be staying in India?'

'Oh Pete, I'm still not sure. I love you so much, and of course that has made me question my original intention to make a new life in India.'

'I can feel a 'but' coming on,' he replied fatalistically.

'Well, I still feel that I need to spend some time in Kolkata, meeting my Indian family and getting to know my mother, or at least what she had been like. I'm sorry but until I have done that, I don't feel I can make any firm decisions as to what comes next.'

'I know, but promise me this, that you will remember that I love you, and if you're willing, I want to spend the rest of my life with you. Marry me, Meera.'

'Oh Pete,' she whispered, 'I love you too, you know I do, but I just can't make any promises right now.'

'Well, I know you intend to stay in India for a month before coming back to sort out your affairs here. When you do, I'll be waiting for you, and for your answer.'

With that, they made love again. For Pete it was a promise of eternal love. For Meera it was an expression of her feelings at that moment.

Four days later Meera was looking down on England from the window of the Emirates flight to Dubai, where they would pick up the flight to Kolkata airport. As the green fields of England disappeared, to be replaced by the choppy waters of the Channel, she was reflecting on all that had happened. Sunita's ashes were inside the cabin luggage in the locker above her head, finally on their way home to India.

Now though, as her thoughts turned to Pete, she was unsure whether her new life would, after all, be in India. He had looked so forlorn when she glanced back at him as she followed her aunt and uncle through to the departure lounge. When he saw her looking, he waved and gave a broad smile. Her heart went out to him. In the last ten days he had given her more affection and love than she'd experienced in her whole life. Could she live her life without him?

She didn't know, she only knew that her life from now on would be very different from the one she had been living only a few short months ago, on the day she'd made the decision to use the Old St Paul's site for her project.

Now, she wonders whether that had been her decision alone or whether other forces had been at work on that day?

Author Bio

Marilyn Freeman

Born in the industrial town of Oldham, Marilyn initially forged her path as an Industrial Chemist, delving into the intricacies of science. In the later chapters of her life, Marilyn discovered a passion for storytelling. Five years ago, she embarked on a writing career that has seen the publication of five novels. Four of these books belong to the captivating genre of family mystery and suspense, highlighting Marilyn's skill in crafting tales that grip the reader's imagination.

Marilyn's fascination lies in the intricate dance of characters within her stories. She delves into the complexities of human relationships, unearthing the profound repercussions of choices that resonate through generations. In her writing, she skilfully navigates the twists and turns of familial ties, unravelling the mysteries of the human heart.

As Marilyn Freeman continues to add chapters to her life's story, her passion for storytelling remains undiminished. Through her novels, she invites readers to join her on a journey through time and emotion, where the threads of family, mystery, and suspense are expertly woven into a tapestry that captivates the imagination.

Find Marilyn's other books at: https://marilynfreemanbooks.com